THE ORDEAL OF BARATÁ

THE ORDEAL OF BARATÁ

A Political Fantasy

by

S. FOWLER WRIGHT

THE BORGO PRESS

An Imprint of Wildside Press LLC

MMX

CONTENTS

PRELUDE

BARATÁ, as we all know, is a small Central American republic on the northeastern seaboard of that mysterious continent, and no ordinary newspaper reader can be ignorant of the acute trouble which broke out in the early part of last year between it and Bioli, its northern neighbour.

It is common knowledge also that the immediate occasion, if not the originating cause, of that demonstration of hostility was the public assassination of an official representative of Baratá in the public gardens of Bioli's capital city; but the circumstances of this tragic and momentous crime were, from their nature, a secret closely kept, and strenuously denied. It is only now, after the discord has died away, and the United States has ceased to consider the necessity of landing marines to persuade the two yapping members of its troublesome Central American kennel to a sulky peace, that the whole tale can be frankly told, without fear of contradiction or consequence, especially as His Excellency Señor Serati, in whose fertile amoral mind the scheme which consigned Dr. Enrico Dalston to so dramatic an end had its inception, is no longer living.

CHAPTER ONE

THE QUESTION OF WHERE THEY SIT

THE head steward of a modern liner has no more delicate duty than the allocation of the passengers' seats in the dining-saloon. This is true of the ocean liners of every nationality and all parts of the world, but most particularly so of those which serve the jealous and excitable citizens of Latin America.

The operation is somewhat facilitated by the custom of inviting the passengers to seat themselves in informal promiscuity for the first meal, giving time for the head steward to study the passenger-lists, and for some casual acquaintances to be made, before they file into the saloon, and are invited, one by one, to inspect the plan of the tables, and express any preferences which they may have already formed.

Those who are seated together for fifty or a hundred consecutive meals will either develop a friendly intimacy which blooms into most sudden flower, as plants may do in the shorter summer of the moon (and which will fade with an equal suddenness when the short voyage is done), or be roused to antipathy, or reduced to resentful boredom, if they be associated with those who are uncongenial or discordant in opinions, or age, or habits, so that the harmony of the voyage is very largely dependent upon the discretion with which these allocations are made.

Apart from that, there are questions of social precedence, often difficult to resolve, and concerning which it is of the first importance that no serious mistake should be made.

To the envious glance of a steerage passenger, the empty first-class dining-saloon might appear to be indistinguishable in desirability, and its scattered tables, alike in their shining appointments, to be of an equal glory. But that is far from the fact. There is the captain's table. There is that of the chief engineer. There is the one over which the ship's doctor presides. There are small tables for one or two only which accommodate those who are not inclined for sociability, and also—and of more importance—those who regard themselves as of an eminence with which the head steward does not agree, though he is shrewd enough to know what they will expect. The seats at the captain's table are already filled. To place them with less prominent companions may be to lose a good tip at the end of the voyage. It may mean that they will transfer their patronage to a rival line. He offers them a table *à deux*, which, though with no gratitude, they must accept. They understand that they are not graded, but placed apart.

The head steward of the *Abasco* (just out of Southampton, for San Luíz, San Collona, Rio, Buenos Aires, and other South American ports) thought he saw a way through his greatest difficulty, if he would omit his usual precaution. There were seven available seats at the captain's table. His practice was to allot six, and keep one in reserve, to which he could transfer a passenger whose importance had been overlooked if a later need should arise. It was a habit private to his own mind, and those of his immediate staff, for the dinning-tables are rarely filled on the first day out, even though the sea may be as smooth as an inland lake on a windless day.

But this time there were, at the least, seven whom he could not place elsewhere without almost certain offence. There was Dr. Enrico Dalston approaching him now.

There was no doubt where he must sit. Up to a few months ago his father had been Chairman of the Line. The death of Sir Miles Dalston had shown him to have amassed one of the largest fortunes that the shipping industry had ever provided for a private pocket. He had not been a mere owner of ships, but a "magnate" in the financial columns of the daily Press. His son had inherited a seat on the board of the S.A.A. Line. More than that, he had been left an actual majority of the Company's shares. In ultimate, if unexercised, power, he controlled the Line.

But rumour said that he was less interested in shipping than in the profession in which he had taken his degree shortly before his father died; and having inherited such wealth, and the freedom which it gives, it was not surprising that he had booked a passage to Baratá, for it was his mother's land, and he had himself been born in the adjoining republic of Bioli, though they were countries which, since infancy, he had never seen. His father had never liked them. His mother, exiled at the call of love, had talked of them ceaselessly to her only child, when her husband had not been within hearing. To the boy's imagination they had become a paradise of celestial beauty, the real home to which, with his mother's infective yearning, he longed to go. And so, having taken his diploma, and with no ties in the Old World which it would not be easy to break, he had decided to go.

The head steward saw a young man approach who was lean and tall, and with more beauty of face and form than is usual to the men of his father's race, but that race was unmistakably shown in the direct gaze and friendly frankness of the grey eyes, and in a perfection of English speech natural to one who had heard it spoken around him from his third year. It was equally natural that he should be proficient in the language which he had learnt from his mother's lips, and in which she had been accustomed, until her death three years before, to talk always to him when they were alone together.

The head steward pointed to the chart. "Number two, sir, if you please," he said deferentially.

The first seat on the right of the captain's chair had a name entered against it already: *Señorita J. Gómez.* The next beyond it was to be Dr. Dalston's. The head steward did not suppose that he would object to that. His watchful assistant was already making out the card. In another moment, Dr. Dalston's name would have been entered on the chart.

But he said pleasantly: "If there's room at the doctor's table—?" And the head steward, concealing a momentary surprise, gave him the seat which he preferred. He thought, with satisfaction, that he might be able to reserve the allocated seat, as his habit was, which it had seemed that he would be unable to do.

CHAPTER TWO

A COMPANION OF JULIANA

DR. DALSTON had been moved by no impulse of humility. He had no desire or expectation of hearing Captain Spotley's voice say: "Friend, come up higher," as the parable foretells to be the fate of those who seat themselves on too low a bench.

He had chosen the doctor's table because he was keen to discuss a subject on which a ship's doctor, travelling regularly between English and South American ports, would be likely to be well informed. He had already given some special study to the wonders of the South American flora, which have provided so many new (and perilous) drugs for European pharmaceutical use. Where so many had been found already, might there not be others of equal potency to be discovered by one who had studied botany, had command of great wealth, and might find ways to the confidence even of the pure Indian tribes, as a man of wholly European ancestry would be unable to do?

So he dreamed. But it is given to few to map the course of their lives accurately for future years, except they be content to walk in much-trodden paths. There will be so many obstacles to be overcome, so many lures to call them aside. The strongest will may need the alliance of happy chance if it is to arrive at its distant goal.

Even in his choice of the doctor's table Enrico Dalston found that he had nursed a most sterile hope. His medical colleague knew so little of South American flora, or the origin of the drugs which he dispensed for sickness upon the voyage, that it would have been difficult, if not impossible, for him to have cared less. Nor were opportunities of conversation at the dinner-table such that his ignorance need be indecently bared.

Dr. Robey was a good-humoured, ease-loving man, who had disposed of an outlying country practice because he objected to turning out during the night. He had used a relative's influence to get him the appointment he now held, because, though he might still be liable to be called during the night hours, such occasions would be few, and it was certain that he would not have to go far.

He enjoyed presiding at his table, for which he had a stock of stories and jests which might not be very extensive, but was sufficient for the few weeks during which a single audience would remain to hear them. After that, they could be recommenced with the pleasant certainty that they would be greeted with the same laughter as before.

The head steward knew Dr. Robey's stories. He knew the kind of people who would appreciate them, who were also the kind that the doctor liked to see seated around him. With the insight of long experience he glanced at each passenger as he appeared, and selected those who would find the doctor's conversation congenial. They might not thank him for putting them at that table, but at the end of the voyage they would be content that they had had a good time, and it is the final verdict that counts. But if they took a second voyage on the *Abasco* they would be seated elsewhere, lest the doctor should be silenced, or they bored by hearing his stories a second time.

Now, Dr. Robey knew who Dr. Dalston was, and would have been willing, though scarcely anxious, to please one of his importance, for was he not practically his employer?—though he took life too easily to disturb himself much, even for that. But he saw only a pleasant-mannered colleague, much younger than himself, who showed a ready disposition to become silent, and let the light-hearted chatter go its own way, which tended to ribaldry before the dessert appeared.

The other occupants of the table were middle-aged people of the hard-drinking, broad-joking types, with which Dr. Robey was most at ease. The head steward understood that single ladies were not to be sent to his board, unless they were such as would be unlikely to ask for a jest to be explained, which it was not always seemly to do. Listening, watching, smiling, answering readily any remark addressed to himself as good companionship required, Enrico saw that he had made a mistake. But it was not one which he had thought of disturbing until he saw Juliana at the captain's table next morning, and learned what he had missed.

At that time he was alone at his table, and she at hers. There was nothing surprising in that. Lunch and dinner on the *Abasco* were at set hours, for which a bugle was sounded about the ship. But breakfast was a meal to which each passenger would come (if at all) at his own time. On the first day out, with a fresh wind abeam giving the liner a slight but perceptible roll, there were many who would not come. Only the young and vigorous, such of them as were not vexed by the tossing waves, would appear at 8:30 A.M. when the saloon was opened. But Enrico, entering at five minutes after the hour, saw nothing surprising in the fact that Juliana was already there. She was five years younger than he, and of a vitality which would be unlikely to miss a meal for any presumption of heaving sea.

They faced each other for that meal over a bare space, though they were three tables apart. They had opportunities of studying one another which they did not miss. Enrico's breakfast took longer in consequence, though he ate less. Juliana's took longer still, for she ate more.

But he sat on until she rose and left, and after that he sought the purser, and enquired who she was.

That was easily told. She was a young lady of Bioli who had been educated in England, and was now on the way back to her native land. She was travelling alone.

Five years before, she had come to England on the *Abasco*, being then in the charge of an older woman. The purser said that she was little changed. He shared a memory of a vital, vivid, impulsive girl, with some length of leg, which had been more freely shown than it was now. It was evident that she was a young lady of whom he approved.

But it was not because he approved of black hair with a natural curl and a natural gloss, or of eyes that were equally bright and dark, or the pale Spanish beauty of an oval face, or the joyous vitality which was more than any of these, that he had seated her at Captain Spotley's right hand. He knew better than that.

It was because she was the daughter—actually the only child— of President Gómez, who ruled Bioli more absolutely than most twentieth-century kings would attempt to do.

In Central and South America, presidents come and go, and before they come they are mostly of small account, and of still less when they are gone. But while they remain in power they, and their only daughters, have a status which must not be lightly ignored. The head steward had placed her where he considered she had a right to be, and no less readily because he saw that neither Captain Spotley nor Dr. Dalston would be likely to complain of the selection which he had made.

The purser asked, would Dr. Dalston like an introduction to be arranged? Dr. Dalston thought not. He had discretion to prefer the less formal approach. But he considered how he could recover the position at her side which he had so ignorantly thrown away. It was a point on which he would not be easily foiled, but which yet seemed a formidable difficulty, for, though he might have the power to secure his will, it was that which he would be reluctant to use. Certainly not in a way which would require rudeness to another passenger.

When next he saw the head steward hurrying past, he stopped a deferential man, and approached the subject tentatively with a remark that he supposed that few of the dining-tables were full. That was no more than to state the obvious, the ship carrying about half her full complement of first-class passengers.

But the head steward had had a hint from the purser, and came to the point at once. "There's still your seat at the captain's table waiting for you, if you'd like to have it."

"Seat number two, was it not?"

"Yes, sir. Between Señorita Gómez and Madame Marthe."

"Very well. You can transfer me to that."

Enrico strolled away, thanking Fate, as he had some reason to do, though perhaps not overmuch. It could afford to give him a free pass in the courts of love, having prepared for him a peril of another kind. With no foresight of this he took the good that came with a glad hand. He had already resolved that Juliana was the most desirable prize that the world held, but that realisation made him the more cautious in his approach. He had three weeks ahead. If he sought her now she might avoid, even resent, a too-obvious pursuit. He would wait till lunch-time, when acquaintance might be naturally made.

He did wisely in that, for though he had been more in Juliana's thoughts than she would have been likely to own, she would have been more wary for that, having in mind the letter which she had had from her father a week before, in which he had warned her against the facile shipboard friendships which so seldom come to a lasting fruit, but which may entangle a girl in ways which are easier to regret than to cast aside. To that letter she had sent a gaily confident reply, and she was in no mood now to lose sleep for the first stranger who looked at her with admiring eyes. Everyone looked at her, and they were few indeed who were content with a single glance. She would have been saint, or pure fool, if she had not been conscious of that.

But when she came to lunch and found Dr. Dalston already occupying the next seat, she was not greatly annoyed.

CHAPTER THREE

"The Space That Makes Attraction Felt"

THE minutes passed, and they were still the sole occupants of the table, a circumstance which seemed singular in itself, and gave to their position an intimacy, if not a significance, which it would not otherwise have held.

"I hope," he said, "that my coming here hasn't frightened everyone else away."

"It does look rather like it," she agreed, and then, fearing a note of rudeness in that assent, added: "It hasn't frightened me."

"Perhaps," he countered lightly, "you didn't know I should be here."

She was audacious in her reply, guessing what she did: "I hadn't any idea. Why did you come?"

"As a matter of fact, it is the seat that was allotted to me, but I tried the doctor's table. I came because I like the best society I can get."

"Then it's a shame that they're not here."

"Do I look very depressed?"

"No, I can't say you do."

"Perhaps I know when I'm well off."

She hesitated on a retort which must have brought an even more direct compliment to herself, and changed to: "I'm told the captain doesn't often come down to lunch."

"That doesn't account for all the seats being empty while the other tables are filling up."

"No. I suppose one or two more will be turning up before long."

"Do you know who the others are?"

"I've heard their names. There are Señor Serati, the Baratá Minister of Health, and his secretary for two. "

"Señor Serati is a gentleman I shall be happy to meet. "

"Yes?" she said dubiously. "You know him?"

"No. But I shall be glad to have the opportunity."

She laughed lightly, repeating the tentative "Yes?" and adding: "I don't think many are."

"I am a doctor myself, and am on the way to Baratá."

"Doctor? Oh, I see. You mean because he's Minister of Health! It's the health of President Cortéz he looks after. I don't think he's much good for anyone's health besides his."

It was a remark from which Enrico concluded, naturally enough, that Señor Serati acted as private medical adviser to his country's ruler. It was a narrow interpretation of the duties of a Minister of Health, but he knew that there is a difference between the political customs of Europe and Central America, which he must be prepared to accept without unfriendly comment if he were to establish himself in his mother's land.

None too soon, Señorita Gómez had reminded herself that she was no longer an irresponsible girl, but the daughter of Bioli's president, and that careless words may be repeated in inflammable ways. She added: "But you won't see either of them. Señor Serati, or so I am told, always prefers to take his meals in his own suite, though there have to be places kept empty here, in case he alters his mind; and his man Pedro never leaves him for more than a few yards. There's a Madame Marthe at your other side. She's the mother of someone important in Argentine. She's not up yet. And the other three are a Chilean envoy to somewhere in Europe, with his wife and a lady cousin. He's returning to Chile on six months' leave. I suppose they'll fly over the Andes. Now you see what a dull lot we are. I should think you'll go back to the doctor's table, and give them another chance there."

Her voice had sunk on the declaration of the dullness of her table companions with the realisation that the three Chileans had entered the room, and were not more than a couple of yards away.

Mutual introduction of some formality followed, and the conversation became general. Before the meal concluded, the Chilean envoy, a brisk, rather consequential man, more concerned to boast the vigour of his receding youth than his diplomatic capacities, had challenged Enrico and Juliana to a deck-tennis contest, with his cousin, a rather bony spinster, as his own partner. His wife. a broadly built, lethargic woman, accepted this arrangement with satisfaction. She went to sleep after lunch herself, which she said was the only sensible thing to do.

The game was new to Juliana, and, at first, experience turned the scale. The Chileans won. But at the end of an hour of keen, good-tempered contest, on a deck which sometimes rolled disconcertingly to a lifting sea, the tide of success turned. The defeated pair, retiring in some exhaustion on the excuse of the tea that the deck-steward was handing round, while their opponents were still fresh in the effrontery of youthful vigour, issued a challenge to a return match. Enrico accepted it for his partner and himself with informal alacrity. Such a partnership may not lead to another of greater permanency, but it is a step on the longer road.

From that time, during the weeks which passed before the *Abasco* cast anchor outside San Luíz harbour, they became a recognised pair who played together at the deck-sports which were pursued with a more general avidity as the ship steamed under warmer skies, and they were not easy to match. Those who watched assumed that their companionship must come to more than, to Enrico at least, it seemed sure that it would. There would have been little surprise had an engagement been announced. But Enrico found, in spite of all the joyous friendship she gave in a comradeship which was sometimes almost continual from dawn to dusk, that there was a barrier he could not peaceably pass, and he feared to venture the violent assault which must have broken it down, or repulsed him to the loss of all he already had.

He found that he must continue a quiet siege, or risk more than he would be willing to lose.

It may have been a prudence he need not have used. It is certain that Juliana was not indifferent to him. If he did not fill her dreams, it may have been because no recollected dreaming survived from her healthy sleep. That she was gaily baffling to any sentimental approach may have arisen from an instinctive fear that, if she should allow the outer barrier to be broken through, the inner would be too quick to fall. So the days passed.

Although Juliana's instinctive reaction to this sea-voyage friendship was to maintain her own integrity from abrupt surrender, perhaps influenced in this more than she was aware by the warning with which her father had fortified her (for who would wish to do that which has been foretold as a youthful folly into which all young girls who adventure unchaperoned travel will be certain to fall?), another instinct, more fundamental, though perhaps no more conscious in its operation, watched that she should not lose that which she was unready to take.

When Enrico mentioned the long-cherished purpose he had to make his home in his mother's land, where he hoped to find scope for medical practice and research, she was probingly sceptical of the strength of this boyhood's dream. "You will not be long there," she said, "at a good guess. You are too English for that. You will find the people of Baratá will not be easy to understand."

But seeing that his purpose was not to be lightly turned, she praised Bioli, as an even fairer, more desirable land.

He was not concerned to deny that. He mentioned that he had actually been born in Bioli, though his mother's country was Baratá.

"Well," she said, "you should see both. I suppose you have booked a passage to San Collona?"

"Yes. But that is no matter, if you can tell me a better way."

"There is no shorter way to San Cristóval, if you mean that. But some people leave the ship at San Luíz, and see Bioli first. They go to San Cristóval overland. The railway is good enough. I would not say more. But I have not seen it for five years. It may have improved. It goes up to the mines, and then down on the other side of the river through Baratá. It is the way the mountains can best be seen, and the forest, which is still wild. The railway goes inland to the mines, through a forest where there are no roads."

"It is at San Luíz that you will land?"

"Well, of course! But that is no reason for you. I am telling you how the country can best be seen."

"I think it will be an excellent plan."

"I must tell you that you will have to make a short stay in San Sebastián. It may be for no more than a few hours, or it may be for as much as two days or three. It will depend upon when the train starts for the hills. But the palazzo is large. My father will welcome so distinguished a guest. I tell you that because when you land at San Luíz you will be pestered by louts, and might be persuaded to book an hotel from there, which it would be needless to do."

"It is very kind of you to say that. It is an invitation I shall not be likely to refuse or forget."

He spoke with the satisfaction of one who sees a step farther ahead on a doubtful road, but he was still uncertain how much or little this friendly invitation might mean. It might be no more than the hospitality which is often given in a strange land to those who come with well-accredited names. Perhaps, by the customs of Bioli, the only significance would have been in such a word having been left unspoken!

But there was no doubt that he would prefer to approach San Cristóval from Bioli, which had not been his previous intention.

Juliana also was well content. She seemed to have dismissed the subject casually from her mind as she rose hastily from the lunch-table where the conversation had taken place. "If we are quick," she said, "we shall get the quoits before those wretched Alvanzos finish their cigarettes."

CHAPTER FOUR

APPROACH ONA SUMMER SEA

THE sea was as smooth as glass: the sky was brilliant with tropic stars.

The passengers of the *Abasco*, after three weeks of segregation from their customary routines and occupations, were beginning to stir restlessly in anticipation of the approaching shore.

Emotional and inexperienced travellers exchanged addresses with those to whom they would not have spoken under conditions other than this enforced propinquity; experienced ones recommended or damned hotels. The sports deck had become neglected, even during the comparatively cool, early morning hours. Those passengers who were disembarking had lined the rails watching for land. Their talk had been of customs' duties, of language difficulties, of stewards' tips. They had exchanged hints regarding cosmetics; they had told fearful legends of insect pests.

Midnight neared as Enrico sat on the upper deck beside two men who, with stretched legs, and glasses beside their hands, engaged in such tentative conversation as affinity of situation, rather than a less superficial congeniality, will allow.

They had, in fact, seen about as little of each other during the past three weeks as had been possible to those who travelled in the same class, Señor Serati and his secretary having remained, even for meals, in the seclusion of his private suite, as he considered necessary to the dignity of a member of the Government of Baratá, emerging only in the cool of the evening hours for the air and exercise which even important Ministers of Health of Central American republics are required by Nature to take, during which hours, as most others, Enrico had a companionship more attractive than that of Señor Serati would be likely to prove.

Even at this last opportunity, though having a purpose in what he did, it is unlikely that he would have been seated there had not Juliana retired early to her cabin with an emphatic refusal to reappear till the next day. Could he not understand how much packing she would have to do?

It is pleasant to have a father who will provide sufficient funds for the purchase of twenty frocks before you leave Regent Street indefinitely behind (most of which you don't intend to unpack till you get home, but about which you alter your mind on the way), but it does mean that your packing, even with the help of a willing stewardess, will be a greater nuisance than is that of less fortunate passengers.

"Señor," Enrico asked after a time, having introduced himself an hour before for the sole purpose of this question, "could you tell me whether there would be good prospects for a doctor, with satisfactory English credentials, who should settle in Bioli or Baratá?"

The dusk of the tropic night hid the stare of perhaps natural astonishment with which this question was received.

"Señor, do you ask this for yourself, or for a friend whom you may be desirous to help?"

"Oh, for myself! I am hoping to make it my settled home."

For the first time, Señor Serati regarded the young English doctor in a personal manner. He saw it to be a natural question to be addressed to himself, he holding the office of Minister of Health in the country where Dr. Dalston was proposing to practise; though he may have had as little medical knowledge as any man among the *Abasco*'s passengers, his actual duties being those of a Chief of Police, for which office President Cortéz, who had a sense of humour, had said: "I have given you the title that you should have, for you can safeguard my health in no better way."

In this ministerial capacity he had become exactly aware of the number of British citizens who had seen reason to settle in Baratá. There were three of these, of whom one was the British Consul, and the other two were fugitives from justice, who would not be extradited so long as they had money to spend for his own and his country's good. But why should any English doctor—and especially this one—be anxious to settle there?

The duties of his position might not have familiarised Señor Serati with the details of medical practice, but they had trained him to be alert and accurate in his observations of those about him. This young doctor, of whose wealth he was well aware—for there was little of the ship's gossip which had not been brought by his own body-guard to his private suite—was certainly not a fugitive from indignant law. He had a buoyant manner, not suggestive of one who fled from the scene of a hopeless love. He had a given name which is not commonly heard in the British Isles. He spoke Spanish—a corrupt form of which is the language of Baratá—with noticeable fluency and idiom. There was something here of mystery into which a Minister of Health, as President Cortéz interpreted the duties of that office, should not omit to enquire, and on which he had, in fact, become fully informed. He avoided direct reply to ask: "It is your first visit to the New World?"

"No. I was born in Bioli. But as I was under three when I was taken to England, you will understand that my recollections are not very useful now."

"Bioli is not Baratá."

"Yes. I understand that! I am told that you are neighbours between whom there is little love. But my own preference is for Baratá."

"Yet it is in Bioli that you were born, and it is there that you are electing to land?"

"I thought that I would see something of that country first, before travelling inland to San Cristóval."

"But if you like that which you see first, you may change your mind?"

"Oh, no! I shall come. You see, Baratá was my mother's land. It is where I have always longed to be, and where I am most likely to settle down. That is, if I find a sufficient welcome for a doctor who is half English, and has been trained in the English schools."

"But—pardon me, Doctor, if I am wrong—to practise your profession is not—how do you say?—is not needful to you?"

"I am not exactly a poor man, if you mean that. But I adopted my profession from choice. It is the first interest that I have. And next to that, it is my wish to make my home in the land that my mother loved, and to which she always hoped to return."

"Well, if you remain of that mind, I daresay you will find practice enough."

Dr. Dalston replied modestly that he hoped he might, but he recognised that the diseases of tropic lands must differ from those of which he had had most experience. He would have developed the conversation from that point, thinking that a Minister of Health should be able to tell him much more that it would be useful to know, but he found Señor Serati to be so vague, or else so startling in his replies, that he concluded, beyond the fact, that he was proposing to enter a land in which the practice of medicine was in a very primitive stage.

He changed the subject slightly to talk of the great debt that European pharmacy owes to the South American continent for a score of its most potent drugs. He suggested that, for one discovered secret of its bewildering flora, there must be a hundred unguessed that the forests hold.

He mentioned a plant of which his mother had told him the name, to which strange virtues were ascribed by Amazonian tribes. He hoped to investigate that.

"Then you must go a thousand miles farther south," Señor Serati replied. "You will find that plant to be as rare as a woman's virtue in Bioli or Baratá."

Enrico Dalston was surprised at this disparaging simile, and, being a young and chivalrous man, felt some inclination to resent so general a reflection upon the women both of his mother's land and of that in which Juliana was born. But he considered that Baratá was the speaker's own country also, and he did not suppose the comparison to be very seriously intended.

"I suppose," he replied, "you go beyond what you would have me believe when you say that?"

"As to the virtue of the women of Baratá? Oh, it is no more than a jesting proverb we have! But I would not say it is widely wrong."

"Perhaps you have been unfortunate in the ladies whose acquaintance you have had the honour to have."

Señor Serati stared for a second time, and the expression of his face was hidden once more by the friendly night. He felt vaguely that he was rebuked, which was an experience he did not lightly endure, and he was genuinely puzzled by a remark which sounded absurd. Surely, if the ladies he had known had been of surrendering moods, unfortunate was not the word, but rather its opposite, which should be applied to his resultant experiences!

"If you would settle in Baratá," he said, "you should not omit to call on President Cortéz when you arrive. I will recommend you to him. "These words were well enough, but they were spoken abruptly, closing the conversation in a curt manner. Having said them, he addressed his companion: "Come, Pedro. The air chills." Without waiting for Dr. Dalston's reply, he got up. He had decided that he was a young man whom he would not like.

Enrico watched his rather paunchy figure disappear, with the taller Pedro keeping at his side, and yet slightly in the rear, as respect required. He felt that he had spoken foolishly, making a point of that which an Englishman would have passed in silence, or not noticed at all. It was, he supposed, a defect of his mother's blood. Yet defect, in that connection, was a word of which he should not think. And particularly not so at this moment, when he was coming to the longed-for home of his childhood's dreams. Was it not rather the English side of his nature which he must be alert to criticise or subdue? It was a difficult decision, for on the one side was a love that was half a dream, and on the other a more rational pride.

But he was sure of one thing. This Minister of Health, who was so singularly ignorant of the elements of medical science, was a man with whom he had no inclination for more intimate acquaintance. Yet, at the moment, his example was good. He rose, with the lithe, almost panther-like lightness which was a legacy of his mixed blood, and curiously variant from the level steadiness of his voice, and the direct gaze of his English eyes, and went down to his cabin.

CHAPTER FIVE

BIOLI INTENDS WAR?

AS the dawn came, the *Abasco* lay-to at the entrance of the harbour of San Luíz, which is the best that Bioli has, but yet not deep enough to be entered by a ship of 19,000 tons, nor to give safe anchorage against the force of a northeast gale. Those who landed here must be taken off by a smaller vessel which had bustled out when the lights of the *Abasco* had been seen far off in the dusk of dawn.

They proceeded inland to San Sebastián, the capital city, by a railway of a wider gauge than that which went from there inland to the mines, and down the Baratá side of the estuary to San Cristóval, and on to San Collona, the best port for three hundred miles, either north or south.

Being situated at the mouth of the river which divided the two republics, its possession enabled Baratá to levy customs duties upon the metal ore which was the main export of Bioli, even though the undisputed Biolian territory on the northern side of the river was not more than a quarter of a mile away. Yet what, beyond curses, could it be profitable to say? The inhabitants of Bioli were about 300,000 of sundry sorts. Those of Baratá were two-thirds of a million. Baratá possessed an old destroyer, one more or less airworthy bomber, and two batteries of quick-firing guns. Against these formidable exhibits, Bioli's arsenal was discreetly veiled.

Enrico, being entertained by President Gómez with the hospitality which Juliana had promised, soon had evidence of the bitter feeling which divided the two republics. He had been warmly welcomed for his English nationality, for his birth-claim to Bioli, and perhaps not least for himself. But when he had mentioned his mother's nationality, and his intention of proceeding to Baratá, he was met by a reserve, a coldness, or at best an effort to dissuade him which seemed to go beyond the etiquette of hospitality.

Unreluctantly, he accepted a warmly pressed invitation from the President himself that he should at least prolong his visit sufficiently to see what Bioli could offer for his admiration, either of natural beauty or human art. He did this without assurance of how far Juliana might have inspired the invitation, or even approve his extended stay, for since his arrival in San Sebastián she had withdrawn herself from more than the friendly impersonal contacts which she must maintain with any guest in her father's palace.

She may have done this with no further object than to demonstrate to her father's eyes that she had no lively interest in the casual traveller to whom she had shown a courtesy due from the President's daughter to a distinguished stranger who visited Bioli, and who had travelled from England on the same ship as herself. She may have felt that she had her prey so securely hooked that she could afford to slacken the line. She may have been observing no more than the reserve which is considered an obligation of modesty in the tropic countries of the New World. She may have thought that the time had come when Enrico should approach her father rather than herself, if he were serious in the advances which he had already made. He saw that her conduct could be interpreted in many ways, all of which were not unfavourable to him. But he was unsure, and his English training inclined him to arrive at a direct understanding with her before he should ask what he supposed would be no more than the formality of her father's consent.

If she fenced, the strain that was in him from his English blood inclined him to meet her with her own weapons, showing himself as independent as she. It was a position he might not have sustained long, but it led him to accept the fact that her time was filled by many social functions, and that she had come home to find many friends, without showing a resentment which must have brought them closer together at once, or made what might have proved to be a permanent breach.

Watchful of its effect, he mentioned at breakfast time, which gave the surest opportunity of personal intercourse, it being often taken by her father and herself together with him as the only guest, that the time had come when he must go on to San Cristóval. Already, a forty-eight hours' invitation had been prolonged to three weeks. President Gómez was polite in his regret, and as urgent that he should prolong his visit as the customs of his country's hospitalities required, but not more than that. Juliana was silent. Enrico, who had been irresolute as to whether he should mention his intention of returning to Bioli, decided that silence was best. He had a reward which he might otherwise have missed when Juliana lingered after her father had left the room, and proposed that he should accompany her next morning, when she would ride into the hills, as she often did before the day came to its full heat.

He had asked for this privilege before, and been lightly rebuffed with the suggestion that the conventions of Bioli forbade.

"Yes," he said, "of course I will come. It is what I have asked before."

She did not affect not to understand the meaning of that.

"As you are leaving tomorrow, it can have no significance, even if it be observed at all."

He thought the logic of that remark (if any) to be of the kind which women proverbially prefer. "It may have no significance," he said, "or else much. It will be as you wish."

There was no displeasure in her eyes as she heard this, and as his own met them he may have had his first moment of confidence that the game was won; but she said no more than to arrange the hour, and dismissed him in the casual manner which she had learnt from her years of English life, rather than from the land of her birth; but they were both, though in different degrees, of the Old World rather than the New, from which the incidence of these first contacts came.

Enrico left with a light heart, being conscious of youth and love and a world of sun. Fate, which was to make him the pawn of a grimmer game, allowed him these days of joy, either as an irrelevance with which it would have been paltry to interfere, or as a contributory factor to the event, shaping him into a readier tool for the use of men whose thoughts were on different things.

He hired a good horse, being fortunately a practised rider at a time when many, even of those with means and leisure, prefer the steering-wheel's inferior joys, and was waiting for Juliana at the appointed hour at the cross-roads beyond the city limits where her prudence, real or assumed, had appointed that they should meet.

She led him by ways she knew far up into the hills, where there was not always space to ride abreast on a narrow path, and they must look first to their horses' feet. There were places which a timid rider would have thought it best to avoid, but they were childhood's custom to her, and there may have been purpose in what she did. They gained wide views of what he could not deny to be a fair land, with San Sebastián a jewel amidst the forest green that flashed white in the sun. He would find that the capital of Baratá, on lower ground nearer the sea, would compare poorly with what he saw.

Conversation on such paths must be intermittent, giving time for thought, and it may be no less pregnant for that.

They thought most of themselves, as youth is likely to do, but Enrico had in mind to question her about some words, not meant for him, which he had overheard the evening before, without knowing that her own thoughts were on the same subject, with the urge of a more definite fear.

The words, if he had caught them correctly, which was not easy to doubt, had been spoken between two members of Bioli's government, and they had implied that war between the two countries was very near, and by the choice of the smaller country, rather than as being thrust upon her.

Well, he had thought, such talk will often die down, as he hoped it might, having no wish to find himself in an atmosphere of machine-gun bullets or bursting bombs. He knew this to be true in all parts of the world, and most particularly so, he supposed, of Central America's excitable semi-Latin populations. Bioli was the weaker state, which should alone be sufficient reason for it to avoid beginning a war which it would be unlikely to win; and, in any case, if it were in earnest, why should it defer the opening of hostilities? He had tried to put the question aside, as a matter of uncertain and probably small significance. He hoped—and indeed expected—that he should find Baratá good-humouredly oblivious of that which its superior strength could safely contemn. It had the coveted harbour, the men, the aeroplane, the guns. Let Bioli talk of what it would do on another day, if it could find satisfaction in that!

Yet he remembered the hostility to Baratá which was latent in every reference he heard, and, perhaps most significant of all, the attitude toward himself which any allusion to his own ties with that land, or intention of settling there, would provoke. He considered what his position toward Juliana would be if war should break out after he had gone. He felt that there was something more than imagination behind his fear, which it might be vital for him to learn.

But, if that were true, he thought that Juliana would know. He had already observed evidences that President Gómez had a great reliance upon his daughter's loyalty and discretion. Young as she was, inexperienced, and having been absent from Bioli during the last five years, it was improbable that he would consult her as one having valuable counsel to give; but she had the confidences of a lonely man.

And he felt sure that there could be no movement of any political importance of which President Gómez would not be aware. Politically, he was Bioli, ruling with an ill-defined, but almost absolute power. He was said to be of an established popularity, and to control his tiny state with an integrity which, if it would not be conspicuous in a more stable world, was above the standard that Latin-American presidents usually observe.

Enrico knew nothing of the ceaseless vigilance, the skilful opportunism, the sometimes ruthlessness by which, for fifteen uneasy years, President Gómez had maintained that unconstitutional temporary throne. But he was right in concluding that, apart from his decision, Bioli could have no plan or purpose of war.

"I heard," he said, as they drew abreast on a level ridge which gave a wide view on the one hand of close-forested hills that fell away to the distant sea, and on the other to yet more distant mountains which, even in that tropic land, were whitened with year-long snow, "something rather startling last night. I heard someone talk as though war between Bioli and Baratá were certain to come."

"There can be few views in the whole world equal to this," she answered, as though she had not heard his remark, which he knew she had, as the next moment showed. He thought there had been a conscious effort at self-control, or the need to decide how she should foil his curiosity, before she replied with the monosyllabic query: "Who?"

"You mean who said it? I don't know that I ought to tell that. I may not have overheard correctly, and, in any case, the words were not meant for me."

She looked more offended than she may have felt as she answered: "You hear words of such a nature as that, and you will not tell me by whom they were said! Are you for Bioli or Baratá?"

He answered with the bluntness of irritation, and the certainty that he had stumbled upon a political secret of some importance: "But, pardon me, that is absurd! Cannot I be friendly with both? Or will you tell me that they are already at war?"

She looked at him, longing to say that which she did not dare. She had meant to warn him, or to persuade him not to go to San Cristóval, and he had made this easy to do, showing that he had heard something of that which she had rightly supposed that he had not guessed, and now the desire to hold her lover warred against loyalty to her father and to her land.

"Have you thought," she said, "that we are far weaker than Baratá? That if they should hear a tale that we are thinking of war, it might be excuse to attack us in the next hour?"

"I don't see why they should attack you at all. What grievance can they have?"

"They have none. The grievance is ours. President Cortéz grows rich on the customs he levies upon our ore. It is what will"—she checked herself, and altered to—"would not last for a week if our strength were equal to theirs."

"So that they might easily be led to suppose that you plan a sudden attempt?"

"I did not say that. They have always regarded us as too weak to be a menace to them. But I meant that you might do more harm than you would expect if you should repeat such talk as that when you are in Baratá. You might start something you could not stop."

"You can be sure I shall not do that. When I am there, I shall say nothing of what I have heard or seen while I have been your guest, for it is plain that you are not friends."

At this point of the conversation, Juliana turned her horse to a downhill path, intending to ride home by another way than that by which they had come. It was a narrow, precipitous descent, where he must follow with care, yet trusting his horse's judgment more than his own, it being familiar with that which was strange to him.

Conversation paused, leaving neither content. Juliana had his assurance that the indiscretion he had overheard would not be repeated in Baratá. From her point of view, there was much in that for her country, but not for herself.

To him, her anxiety for that assurance had brought a puzzled conviction that he had heard no more than the truth, and that Bioli was planning war. Yet the idea had a fantastic sound. He knew enough of the relative strength of the two republics for it to appear a desperate resort. He had heard of no dispute between them beyond this standing grievance, which they had found it possible to endure for several previous years. Most puzzling of all, he had seen no war-like preparations of any kind, and though his observation had not been alert for so improbable a development, he did not think it possible that much could have occurred without his knowledge while he had been the President's guest. He knew that Bioli's regular army, if it could be dignified by that name, was of a nominal strength of 800 men. It was no more than a gaily uniformed presidential guard. Besides that, there was an armed police force, the strength of which was not publicly known. But it was scattered over the country, and its total could not be great. Considering these facts, the whole idea seemed absurd.

He remembered having seen the President and Señor Philipo, the envoy of Baratá, in what had appeared to be a friendly, even jocular conversation, only two days before. He knew enough of diplomatic usage to attach no great importance to that. But the fact remained that he could observe nothing to justify the idea either that Bioli was about to make an attack upon her more powerful neighbour, or that it would be an act of sanity to attempt. He considered that Juliana's youthful inexperience might dispose her to take seriously that which a sounder judgment would discredit, but even this explanation did not satisfy him, perhaps because he understood her too well to believe that she would be so lightly influenced. And if hostilities should be actually about to begin, in which country would he wish to be? He was not doubtful of his answer to that.

As though she had read his mind, Juliana said, as he came to her side again on a level path: "If you believed this silly talk you have heard, would it make no difference to you? Would you still be going to Baratá?"

The question was put so lightly, so teasingly, that he could not tell whether it were seriously meant, or she were using the talk of war as a counter in the game of love which he was more than willing that she should play. He answered in the same vein: "I should not go, if you were to ask me to stay."

"It is nice of you to say that! But you have not answered what I asked."

"No? I thought I had. Perhaps I may make no more than a short visit to Baratá."

"How long do you mean by that?"

"Perhaps a week. Perhaps two."

"It would not be more?"

There was an earnestness in this question which seemed excessive for what it asked, but it showed an interest in his movements which he was not likely to mind. "It need not be more. Do you ask me to promise that?"

"I have no right. Shall you come back here, or return to England direct?"

"You know I am not intending to return to Europe at all. I will come back here, if I am asked."

She looked at him with laughing eyes. "What can I answer to that? I must ask you now, or be rude to a friend, and my father's guest! We shall be most glad to see you again."

"Then you can be sure that I shall be here."

"In two weeks from now?"

"In not more than that."

"And you will forget the silly talk that you overheard, or perhaps misunderstood?"

"I shall not repeat it, if you mean that."

"I am sure you will not."

She turned the conversation next moment in other ways, as one having a carefree mind, nor was there any further allusion to the subject of war with Baratá before he left on the San Cristóval train. He remained in doubt as to what the truth might be, but he felt that she had attached an importance to the limit of his visit to Baratá which suggested a fear, if not a certain knowledge, that there would be trouble between the two countries at a near date. Could she really know that there would be an outbreak of war in the coming month? Or that it would certainly not be within fourteen days? Or had she merely made excuse of what he thought he had overheard to lead the conversation in such a direction that she could obtain his assurance that he would be returning to Bioli?

It was hard to guess. But it was clear, on whatever explanation, that she took an interest in his movements, and would welcome his return to Bioli; and that mattered even more to the egotism of youth than whether the two countries were on the threshold of war.

CHAPTER SIX

THE CURTAIN RISES ON THE EVENT

IT was on the day of Enrico's arrival at San Cristóval, the capital city of Baratá, which is ten miles inland from the port of San Collona, that a conversation took place in President Cortéz's private room, which he would have been interested to hear, though he would have been unlikely to guess how personal its issues would ultimately become.

It was a conversation which had proceeded to a restrained and courteous acrimony among three agitated and angry men.

Señor Philipo, a diplomat small and neat, suave of manner, exact of speech, who held the office of Baratá's envoy at San Sebastián, had left his post two days before to make personal report to his President of that which he would not trust to the written word, and it was not pleasant to hear.

Three months earlier, he had obtained secret information that Bioli had dispatched a mission to the British Government, soliciting a licence for the export of munitions of war sufficient to enable it to feel secure from the armaments of its more powerful neighbour; and, on learning this, President Cortéz had sent his own Minister of Health in the same direction, with instructions to oppose the granting of such a licence, or alternatively, to solicit for his own country the privilege of making similar purchases to an equal value.

From this mission Señor Serati had returned with no better report than that the rebuff he had received had been impartially administered to Bioli also, the British Government saying, with what had appeared to be a polite finality, that it was against its considered policy to supply the means of mutual destruction to the bellicose republics of the New World.

But now it appeared that the issue was worse than that. After Señor Serati had left, the prolonged importunity of Bioli's representative, by whatever argument, had prevailed. It was at least a fact that the moving eloquence with which he had portrayed the defenceless and precarious existence of Bioli beside its better-armed and more populous southern neighbour, had resulted in the issue of a permit to purchase munitions of war to a sufficient amount to place the two republics on an equality of military power.

And the sequel appeared to be even more ominous of approaching trouble. Partly, perhaps, because Bioli's unscrupulous representative may have described the armaments of Baratá as being more considerable than they actually were, and partly because the value of guns of the newest patterns could not easily be assessed against those which had been second-hand when they had been purchased eight years before, the weapons of destruction, which were even now being loaded upon the cargo-boat, *Billy Winch*, at a London dock, would be sufficient to give the army of Bioli what might be no less than a decisive advantage upon the field of battle, and would certainly give its President confidence to commence hostilities.

Indeed, Señor Philipo's information was that an ultimatum requiring the cession of San Collona, and a drastic revision of the customs dues levied upon Bioli's mineral wealth for its use of the only available railway, had already been prepared for presentation, as soon as the expected cargo should have arrived.

"We must not wait for that," President Cortéz said. "We must find a pretext for instant war."

"So we should," Señor Philipo agreed. "But it may not be easy to do."

"Especially," Señor Serati added, "as they will be most careful neither to give nor resent offence till the arms will have arrived."

They gazed at one another in silent consideration of a difficulty not easily to be overcome. They had no grievance against their weaker neighbour. The disputed harbour was in their possession. Should they attack at once with no better excuse than the assertion that they had learned that Bioli had a similar intention at a more opportune time? It would be hard to prove. It might not be believed! And they knew that, in whatever they might do, they must save their face to the world.

This was a matter of special importance to a small maritime Central American republic intending war, for they had always to regard the possible overwhelming intervention of the United States.

Against such interference being capriciously exercised, their only protection, apart from the declared policy of that country itself, lay in the common jealousy of the other republics of Central and South America. But if the fact should appear to be that they were making unprovoked attack against a weaker neighbour, they might find themselves without even diplomatic support against such an eventuality. But they would be in a very different position if Bioli should have acted in a manner provoking war.

"And the time," Señor Serati reflected, "is very short."

"It is not a matter," the President said, "which can be left to chance, or allowed delay. They must commit an outrage upon us during the next week."

"Perhaps," Señor Philipo suggested, "they might sink one of our ships."

The suggestion had a good sound, for the United States, with its own history in mind, could not possibly regard such an incident as an insufficient occasion for war. But President Cortéz frowned. The navy of Baratá was not so numerous that he could contemplate a reduction without regret. A man—even one of his own ministers—could be more cheerfully spared.

"No," he said, "it would be hard to fix it on them. It would tax belief. Have they a submarine? Or even a torpedo-boat that could put to sea? Or a bomber to take the air? It is assassination that it must be."

Señor Serati asked: "How would you charge that to them? They would deny it vehemently. And it would appear an unlikely thing for them to have done. They would demand that an enquiry be held. Would it be a good cause that we should commence war on the next day?"

"That," the President replied, "would depend upon the circumstances surrounding the crime. It must occur in their own land. It must be—" Here he paused, looking at Señor Philipo, and his paunch shook with an inward mirth. "It must be our envoy in San Sebastián. There could be no provocation greater than that!"

Señor Philipo controlled himself to a slight smile.

"Your Excellency," he said, "will always jest."

"Señor Philipo," the President replied, with sobriety in his voice, "it is a sacrifice for your country which it would be to your honour to make."

"It is a sacrifice we should regret," Señor Serati added politely, "but the project is sound—unless, of course, you can think of a better plan."

The diplomat listened to these arguments with an expressionless face. "It might be even better," he suggested, "that it should be one of your more excellent and important selves."

"It is a sacrifice," the Minister of Health somewhat sourly replied, "which I should not refuse to make. But I can see that it would be vain. I am hated by too many criminals here. No one would believe that I had not been assassinated by the malcontent of our own land."

"The crime," President Cortéz decided, avoiding more direct condemnation of the treasonous suggestion that Señor Philipo had made, "must be committed in San Sebastián. There is nothing plainer than that."

"You could visit there."

"The visits of Presidents are not so casually made. It would take time to arrange—and that is what we have not got."

"You could create a precedent of informality."

"And it would be said that I had brought it upon myself: that their police had had no reasonable opportunity to arrange for safeguarding my life, as they would have been active to do."

Señor Philipo could not dispute that. "It is soundly argued," he said, showing his usual diplomatic adroitness in this reply, "and you are also one we could not afford to lose. Beyond that, I can now see that you are right both as to where the crime must occur, and that it must be the envoy of Barată who shall perish, to give the event the importance which we require.

"It is therefore a sacrifice I should not decline, but that I should inflict on my country too great a loss. For, if we go to war, I have a knowledge of Bioli which will be of great value to you. So I will sacrifice myself in a better way. I will resign, so that the appointment may be given to one who will be a smaller loss to Barată and less trouble to you." And, as he heard this, Señor Serati had an idea.

CHAPTER SEVEN

ENRICO DALSTON IS REASONABLY SURPRISED

ENRICO arrived at San Cristóval with a divided mind. It was a fair, white-stoned city, green-cinctured by tropic woods, looking down upon the disputed port, ten miles away, itself a flashing seaside jewel of sand and sun. It was his mother's dream that, with the coming of years of freedom, he would make his home.

But Bioli also had been a fair land, and one to be preferred, even by one whose mother had come of a tropic blood. He had been disposed to remember in the last three weeks, as he had not done previously, that it was there, and not in Baratá, that he had been born.

He recalled the jesting words in which Juliana had described the actual functions of Baratá's Minister of Health, with some advice as to his own procedure in establishing himself professionally, when he had first told her of the object with which he was going to Baratá. "He is not a man." she had said. "who will do anything for you unless he be paid. If you should need his aid in earnest, you would do well to talk to his man, Pedro, who walks behind. He will tell you what Serati will do, and will name the price. At least, that is the talk I have heard. But, at the last, it is President Cortéz who will decide.

"If Cortéz says you can practise in Baratá, you will hear nothing of any law of a contrary kind. You can be sure that there will be none that anyone will be gauche enough to recall. And if he says that he would like you better if you were farther away, all the laws of Baratá will be no protection to you."

He had no longer the same intention, or, at least, not immediately, of establishing himself professionally in Baratá, but he decided that, after spending the remainder of his first day in a leisurely inspection of San Cristóval, he would call upon President Cortéz early on the following morning. It was as the sun was low that he came back to the Hotel of the Seven Saints, and was surprised to find a police officer seated in his private room, who informed him, not without some display of Latin politeness, that he must consider himself under arrest, on a charge that he was a foreign spy.

The accusation sounded so grotesque in its utter baselessness that he found it difficult to regard it seriously. "That," he said, "is absurd."

"I only arrived this morning," he added inconsequently, "from San Sebastián."

"Yes, from Bioli," the police officer agreed, with a sinister look in his yellow eyes.

Enrico saw that he had said the wrong thing. But what right thing could there be to say in refutation of that which had no substance at all?"

I am a British subject," he tried again, "a doctor, travelling on pleasure. I have no connection with your politics. None at all."

"I cannot discuss that. I know only that I have a warrant for your arrest."

The man rose as he spoke. It seemed that his politeness was wearing thin.

"I suppose I can ring up the British envoy?"

"That would be for the President to decide. In the first place, you must come with me."

"Should I bring my luggage?"

"I have no instructions on that. I should say you must leave it here."

"Then where is it that you want me to come?"

"It is to the Presidency that I have to take you. I cannot say beyond that."

That was the first good word he had heard. He had seen the jail, and its odour had been more than sufficient from the outside. But if he were to be taken immediately before someone of sufficient authority—and presumably of intelligence—to deal with whatever accusation had been made against him, it was likely that this exasperating annoyance might soon be over.

"Well," he said, "under protest, I will come with you; but it is an outrage which it will be hard to explain away."

The police officer said nothing to that. He led the way from the room, and down to the entrance hall, where two carbined policemen fell in behind, and they all entered a waiting car, the panels of which bore the two snakes which form Baratá's not inappropriate crest.

Puzzling, while they drove to the Presidency, over this astonishing interference with his personal liberty, he came to the conclusion that it was a blackmailing plot that he would most probably have to meet, and he resolved to resist it with the stubbornness which he had inherited from his father's blood. He recalled his conversation with Baratá's "Minister of Health" three weeks before, and the allusion which Señor Serati had made on that occasion to his reputation for wealth, and he concluded that he had to thank that gentleman's unscrupulous ingenuity for his present experience. It was a surmise which neither did any injustice to the Minister of Health, nor erred widely in regard to the nature of his arrest, but the purpose for which he was required was more subtle than any from which a cheque-book could bring him free.

CHAPTER EIGHT

THE MAGNANIMITY OF PRESIDENT CORTÉZ

DR. DALSTON was conducted to a room that was high and cool. It opened upon a balcony which looked down upon the city, with some more distant view of the river and the disputed shore. It was not a setting which suggested judicial severities, being, in fact, the President's private lounge.

He saw three men there, of whom he knew two. There was Señor Serati, with whom he had parted on the *Abasco's* deck; Señor Philipo, with whom he had talked at a presidential reception in San Sebastián only three days before; and President Cortéz, with whose newspaper photographs he was sufficiently familiar to make a correct guess at his identity.

The President, rolling his bulk in a padded chair, looked at the prisoner who had been brought before him with a good-humoured curiosity, rather than the hostility which would be natural in regarding a foreign spy. He asked: "You are Doctor Enrico Dalston?"

"Yes. I must protest "

"Pardon, Señor!" The President's voice was sharp and authoritative in interruption. "In a moment, I will listen to what you may have to say. But first you will answer me. You are not armed?"

"No. "

"I accept your word." The President's gesture was gracious. "Captain Manuel, you will retire, but remain at call."

On this order, the little escort withdrew. The President waved his hand to a chair. "There is no reason you should not sit."

Enrico took the indicated chair. He looked at three men who seemed in less haste to talk than he was himself, and the idea that he had been brought there to be blackmailed hardened to a conviction. He said firmly: "I should have waited upon your Excellency tomorrow morning, as Señor Serati here had recommended that I should do, but I did not expect that I should be brought here in this outrageous manner."

The President's eyes narrowed. "You were brought here," he said, "on my order, and with all consideration that the occasion allowed. You came here from Bioli, I understand?"

"Yes. There is surely no crime in that."

"You are a native of that country?"

"Only so far that I was born there."

"And Bioli is talking of war with us?"

"If it be so, it is no matter of mine. I am English, that being my father's race."

"And you learned our language from him?"

"My mother was of this country."

"It is among those of such mixed ancestry that spies are most commonly found."

"I told Señor Serati that it was to this country that I intended to come, and to settle here. He will bear witness to that."

He said this less because he regarded it as a point of importance than to test whether the Minister of Health would give a straightforward reply, which he did not expect to hear. But Señor Serati was frank and ready in his response. "That was how I understood it to be."

"Then is it likely I should come here to play the spy? I am a stranger to both countries. I would be friendly to both. I come to practise my own profession." He had almost added: "I am a wealthy man. What could tempt me to such folly?" But he considered that it might be his wealth that they sought to share, and it might be an assertion it would be wiser to avoid. He considered also that, so far, there had not been even a pretence of accusation against him. Nothing more than the suggestion that it was among such as he that spies were found, which amounted to nothing at all. But President Cortéz appeared to be satisfied with his reply.

"Listen to me, Doctor Dalston," he said, with the grave dignity which he had cultivated for such occasions. "Señor Philipo has come here bringing report that you visited San Sebastián, and were taken into the immediate confidence of President Gómez, in a very singular manner. And after visiting him, you come here. We know that Bioli is plotting war, and that they have England's help. You admit that you were born in Bioli, and that you are half English yourself. Can we doubt what has brought you here?"

Listening to this ingenious construction of circumstances with some of which he was familiar, and of which others had a more doubtful sound, Dr. Dalston had his first doubt of whether there might not really be a suspicion against himself, and he was fair enough to recognise that the reason he had given for coming to Baratá, true though it was, might not have a very plausible sound to a sceptical ear. He answered seriously: "I cannot say what Bioli's intentions may be. I was entertained socially, with more kindness than I have met here, but I was not concerned with their politics, of which I heard no more than the most casual talk. But when you say that England is helping them to make war upon you, I am quite sure you are wrong."

"You will say, perhaps, that you have not heard of a cargo boat named the *Billy Winch*?"

"No, I shouldn't say that." He had almost added a further word which might have changed subsequent events in a radical manner, and perhaps saved the lives of more than one who sat there, but a natural caution held him silent, and the President's questions went on.

"You mean that you know the boat?"

"Yes."

"As one flying the English flag?"

"Yes."

"And that it has just left the port of London with a cargo of munitions of war?"

"No, I know nothing of that."

The President did not challenge this denial. He accepted it with a silent gravity. After a pause which appeared to be pregnant with judgment, he said:

"Doctor Dalston, I am disposed to accept your word, and if I do that, I must allow that we have done you an indignity for which reparation must be generously made.

"I do not often own I am wrong, but, when I do, it is to compensate with an open hand. I cannot insult you with gold, which you do not need. I will make a proposition which may surprise you at first, but I will ask you not to reject it until it has been fully discussed."

"I will promise that."

"You have said that you would be friendly both with Bioli and Baratá?"

"Yes, that is how I feel."

"You would avert war, if you could?"

"Yes, I certainly would. "

"So would we. We have much to lose. We have nothing to gain. Would you be our envoy at San Sebastián in place of Señor Philipo, whose health will not allow of the prompt return that the occasion requires?"

Enrico would have said that he was prepared for any possible development after the way in which he had been brought to that room and the conversation which had taken place. He looked upon the three whose eyes were fixed so intently upon himself as no more than powerful and unscrupulous rogues, in which he may not have been widely wrong; and he had not expected to leave that room without learning the method by which they proposed that his wealth should be exploited by them. He had been prepared for almost anything—except what he heard. For a moment, his surprise was beyond control. Then he ordered his thoughts for a reply: "It is an honour for which I must thank you, whether I feel able to accept it or not. And I will not forget that I have promised not to refuse it until it has been discussed. But do you think that I, a stranger, can be fitted for such a post, and at such a time? Or can you trust me so far, having doubted me as you have?"

President Cortéz waved a hand that dismissed doubt. He became somewhat grandiloquent in his reply, though there was more reason in his final words than the Englishman had expected to hear.

"But you must understand that I do not doubt you at all! Had I done so, you would have been shot in the next hour. But I have a judgment that I can trust. Now I think to right a wrong into which I have been led by a lying tale. But, if you think, you will see that all I risk is not much. For if you return to San Sebastián it is certain that you cannot betray us, for you will have had no opportunity of learning anything which it would be useful to Gómez to know. And even if you should be friendly to him, you may have the more potent voice to persuade him to peace, which is what we seek.

"But should you fail, or should you even make no such attempt, we shall have lost nothing at all, for it is a matter in which it is sure that Señor Philipo would not succeed. He would have less chance than one who comes from a neutral land, and can say that he is friendly to all. And I do not doubt that you are sincere, and will do all you can, which may be of great service to us."

Enrico listened to this, which had a plausible sound. He was not sure that he was not being shown the bait of a cunning trap, but he could not see what it could be, and it occurred to him that if these were men whom he should not trust, he could hardly do better than accept an offer which would enable him to return to Bioli, where he could stay if he would, and resign the office when he should be out of reach of the policemen of Baratá.

"It is," he said, "a great surprise that I should have the offer of such a post, and I am far from confident of what I can do. But it is a matter that you should judge better than I, and if you ask me seriously, I will not decline."

"Then you will be doing, "the President answered with gravity, "a great favour to us, and a great service to Baratá."

CHAPTER NINE

THE BREAKFAST TABLE AT SAN SEBASTIÁN

JULIANA was late for breakfast, having taken an hour's ride in the hills as the dawn rose, and President Gómez was earlier than his custom, having had an anxious and wakeful night, so that, when she entered, his meal was almost done.

"You look more worried than ever," she said, as she kissed her father affectionately, "and I can't see why you should. You've got everything moving just as you planned, and I should have thought that you might look just a bit pleased."

"I've been President of Bioli for fifteen years, and I'm not dead yet. The longest time that any previous president lived was four years and a day. If I hadn't worried, do you suppose I should be sitting here now?"

"Yes, I expect you would. You're the best President Bioli has ever had, and they've got the sense to know when they're well off."

"It hasn't been quite as simple as that. It's been partly because they've had something else to hate. There's been the quarrel with Baratá. I haven't ever let them forget that. But it has got beyond control in the end. I had to make a move, which I wasn't anxious to do."

"Well, you've got the arms anyhow. You've won the first trick."

"They're not landed yet."

"But they're on the way in a good boat. That's much the same thing. You don't think Baratá'd try sinking an English ship, even if it knew how."

"Probably not. Though I've not overlooked that. I've no doubt Cortéz would try it on if he dared. But you mayn't be far wrong when you say 'if they knew how.' I don't suppose they've got a torpedo that's less than six years old, or a man who's fired one since rather longer than that. But I have to watch everything. And especially what I don't understand.

"I knew it meant trouble when Philipo slipped away; and I had some very queer news from San Cristóval last night. Very puzzling indeed."

Having said this, President Gómez paused, as though a fresh idea had suddenly come to his mind, so that it obstructed the current of what he had been meaning to say. He added, with apparent inconsequence: "I've thought you looked rather worried at times yourself during the last few days."

"Worried? I?" Juliana's large dark eyes opened in genuine surprise. "I wouldn't say I've got a care in the world, apart from anything troubling you. "

"Well, say you've had something—or someone—more or less on your mind. Enrico Dalston for a first guess."

There was a faint carmine tinge on Juliana's olive cheek as she replied with apparent frankness: "Oh, you meant him? He wasn't bad. He'll be here again soon, more likely than not. I'm not losing weight for him, if you mean that."

"He'll be here tomorrow."

"*Tomorrow!* Then he's soon finished with Baratá! But you're surely not worrying over that?"

The girl looked some surprise but no displeasure at this information, and then her brows drew to a puzzled frown. Had her father reason to think that she was the attraction which was bringing him so suddenly back? And, if so, why should he be worried? Had he not always said that she should make her own choice, without interference from him? And, even for a President's daughter, Dr. Dalston, wealthy, cultured, young, handsome as he was, and half of their Latin blood, could hardly be regarded as an unsuitable selection for her to make.

But the doubt was lost in a surprise of greater magnitude at her father's next words: "He is coming back as Baratá's accredited envoy to us."

"But I thought that Señor Philipo—!"

"He has resigned, and Doctor Dalston is appointed to take his place."

"And that must all have been arranged while he was here!"

It certainly did have that appearance. It seemed impossible that it could have been arranged, without previous discussion, in the few hours that had followed his arrival in Baratá. Señor Philipo must surely have left his post in anticipation that Doctor Dalston would relieve him of it. It gave an aspect almost of duplicity to the promise that he had made, that he would see her again at no distant day.

Or—after all, there had been his duty to Baratá, if it had been a secret that he must not speak! Would it not be fairer to say that he had shown diplomatic reticence of a high order, giving her no hint of the truth, and yet allowing her to anticipate that she might soon see him again? But, even so, everything he had said must be recalled and reconsidered in the light of this startling—and inexplicable—development.

Inexplicable that was the correct, and, to President Gómez, the disquieting word. For he had found that the inexplicable were usually the dangerous things, and that was especially so when they originated in Baratá.

It was true that the fact was not in itself of a sinister complexion, but there was little comfort in that. A sinister move that could be recognised for what it was might be met and foiled on its own ground. But if you could not understand—!

Meanwhile Juliana had recalled some parting words which appeared far from ingenuous on the lips of a man who had expected to return in such a capacity in a few days' time. Suppose he had been making a jest even a tool—of her? Small sharp teeth showed at the thought on a bitten lip. But her tone was cheerful as she echoed her father's words: "Yes, we must see what he has to say."

CHAPTER TEN

THE ATTITUDE OF PRESIDENT GÓMEZ

DR. ENRICO DALSTON, Envoy Extraordinary and Minister Plenipotentiary to the Republic of Bioli, travelled in state. The smaller American republics are jealous of a dignity which, if they should fail in self-assertion, might not be observed by others. He travelled, in fact, in the President's private train, which consisted of a luxurious suite for the use of President Cortéz and his immediate attendants, and another carriage for the armed guard which his safety, as well as his pomp, required. A pilot engine went ahead, which had proved to be a useful precaution on a previous occasion.

There was a separate reason for the use of the presidential train in the fact that it had free running rights over a railway which was owned by a foreign syndicate, which had its head offices in New Orleans. Its use effected a saving of about 15,000 pesos to a treasury which was seldom full.

The railway did not enter at once into Bioli's territory. It did not strike directly for San Sebastián. It commenced its course up the southern bank of the dividing river. For this river, as it neared the sea, opened to a breadth which would have discouraged any project of bridging it, even had the relations of the two republics been more cordial, and their exchanges more considerable.

But farther inland the character of the Aver changed. It flowed between narrow cliffs, in a swift torrent, from a mountainous land. Here it was bridged, and the railway entered Bioli, but still struck upward into the hills, for its goal was less Bioli's capital than Bioli's mines, and its most remunerative traffic was the ore which was brought down to be shipped, for its German owners, from San Collona, the seaport of Barata.

Thirty miles within Bioli's territory, there was a junction where a line branched backward for San Sebastián, but even had the latter port been suitable for shipment of the ore, it would have been impossible to arrange, for the railway had been built under a binding contract that the traffic of the mines should be carried to San Collona.

Enrico Dalston considered these matters in a mind that was pleasantly distracted at times by the outer wonders of what he saw. For the rail, as it left the coast, entered an untamed land, wildly magnificent in its scenery, and clothed in virgin forests which, in some places, must be continually hacked away to maintain a clear track for the trains. He concluded that the position was not one which Bioli was likely to accept for a longer time than it might feel under compulsion to do. Possibly President Cortéz might be making no more than a statesmanlike anticipation of the inevitable, with a wisdom which those in the seats of power too seldom possess.

For the fact was that he had given his new envoy a most generous freedom of negotiation—indeed, so generous that an older and more cynical diplomat might have found it more difficult to believe that it could be genuinely meant. He was to bid for peace, and for Bioli's goodwill, and, to gain that, he might offer reduction of the present customs duties, even to fifty percent, at which figure it could be argued that it would be actually more profitable to use San Collona than Bioli's far inferior port.

Was it surprising that Enrico Dalston, come to this amazing eminence, this splendid opportunity, in a single week, did not dwell upon the disastrous possibilities which are the continual shadow of human fate, or the precarious tenure of life, particularly in Latin lands, but saw himself as the destined saviour and reconciler of the two sister republics from which his own existence derived?

Certainly—as President Cortéz might not have failed to reflect—if he should meet with misadventure in a land to which he came on so magnanimous a mission, it would be a crime of ingratitude to appeal to the whole civilised world. And when the victim would be an English citizen, young, generous, inexperienced, what hope of tolerant sympathy would Bioli have? If Baratá should be swift to chastise her as she would deserve, who would be hardy to intervene? What but further proof of Bioli's nefarious plotting would it be thought, when it should be disclosed that she had a deadly cargo already upon the seas?

Oblivious of such considerations as these, Enrico imagined facile conversations with Bioli's President in which he would offer, in a spirit of conciliation, all or more than might be won by the doubtful hazard of war.

Vaguely, he looked ahead to a time when he might himself be the accepted ruler of Baratá—with the daughter of President Gómez at his side to unite the sympathies of the once-hostile lands. Might he not at last unite them in fact, to a greater strength, a higher destiny, than either could hope to attain alone?

Might he not even go on to further missions of reconciliation and federation, until the whole of South and Central America should become of one single impregnable strength, to which even the United States must defer, as would be pleasant to see?

It did not appear beyond reasonable expectation after what had happened already, that he, with his father's stability of character and capacity for organisation, and his mother's blood, might be the destined protagonist of so great a task.

Bioli and Baratá might be inconsiderable now, both in population and wealth, but their undeveloped resources were quite a different matter, and here again he could be powerful to intervene. The fortune that he had inherited from his father was not less than £1,200,000, even after the huge portion claimed by the English Treasury had been lopped away.

Dreaming thus, he saw the gleaming, sun-drenched roofs of San Sebastián, which he had left reluctantly so few days before. He drove in the luxurious car which had been Señor Philipo's and had become his, to the Legation of which he was now the head, and after a night's rest (for it had been evening when he arrived), he set out to pay the formal call upon President Gómez which the occasion required.

President Gómez received the new envoy of Baratá alone, and with an absence of formality which might be taken in divers ways. Subtle though he was, he did not suspect the plot which was intended to lead to the destruction of Bioli and his own incidental ruin (not that he would have accepted incidental as an appropriate word). His mind went no further on the track of the truth than to perceive that there was something here which he could not guess, and concerning which he must therefore be alert both to discover and to avoid.

It was not his policy of the moment to seek an occasion of quarrel either with Dr. Dalston or Baratá, yet Enrico, even in the first exchanges of mutual civility, was sensible of a different atmosphere from that which had prevailed so pleasantly during his earlier visit.

It was not that he was able to observe an inferior courtesy. Rather, if possible, he was met with a greater scrupulosity of politeness. Nor was there any failure in cordiality. President Gómez had a charm of manner which was lacking in the ruler of Baratá, and this he did not fail to exhibit to one who was both the wealthy Englishman whom his daughter approved, and the accredited envoy of the neighbour republic. But there was an undertone of formality, a reduction of spontaneity, a watchfulness which no technique of courtesy, however practised, could entirely hide. Enrico felt uncomfortably that every word he now said would be measured and weighed, perhaps held to contain significances which he had not meant. How was he, utterly inexperienced in diplomatic exchanges, to acquit himself in this unfamiliar duel?

Wisely, he decided to disclaim a weapon he was untrained to use, and to speak with the simple sincerity which was consonant equally with the impulses of his own nature and the generosity of the instructions he had received.

Endeavouring to lead the conversation to a more real interest than the health of the bulky President of Baratá, he said abruptly: "I hope that the Señorita is well?"

"I am happy to assure you that she is in excellent health."

"I may hope to have the great pleasure of paying my respects to her before I leave?"

"I regret that she is out riding this morning. She will be desolated that it has so unfortunately occurred."

Enrico felt vaguely rebuffed. And he did not fail to observe that Juliana must have known that he had returned to Bioli, and at least anticipated his present call. But he went on to disclose the purpose with which he came, and to use the frankness his instinct urged.

"Excellency," he said, "may I speak to you without reserve, as my inexperience in this office which I have been so unexpectedly asked to accept renders it easiest for me to do?

"I understand that there has been unfriendly feeling between these two countries to which I am almost equally bound by ties either of birth or blood; and I was most surprisingly asked to undertake this appointment, to negotiate a new era of friendship, such as must be advantageous to both. Should I find myself useless for that, I have already resolved that I will resign that which it is probable that I should have been wiser not to accept.

"I will say at once that I am empowered to recognise that there are grievances which must be faced, and to concede much, if it will be accepted with the goodwill which I bring to you."

President Gómez heard this with an expression of smiling courtesy which did not change, and, though his mind became busy with many thoughts, there was no sign of hesitation in his reply.

"You speak," he said, "with a goodwill which I do not doubt, and your words are such as I gladly hear. But will you tell me, with the same frankness as you have already shown, whether you are assured in your own mind that there is such sincerity or goodwill in the hearts of those whose instructions you have received? For you will see that very much will depend on that."

Faced by this question, Enrico had opportunity to observe how dangerous the path of frankness may become, if it be followed too far. He would have liked to reply: "If I know anything of my fellow men, I had my instructions from three of the most unscrupulous rogues that I ever met." He used sufficient, though reduced truth when he said: "You will not ask me to give opinions upon those whom you have known much longer than I. You will consider that I was in San Cristóval for no more than a few hours. But I am empowered to offer you something more substantial than words. Could there be any object in authorising me to negotiate terms which President Cortéz would decline to ratify?"

President Gómez considered this, and the argument had undeniable force. It was Bioli, not Baratá, which had much to gain by three weeks' delay. It was possible that this advance was dictated by prudent fear. Equally possible that it was intended to gain no more time than would enable Baratá to reinforce its own arsenal, so that its fear would cease. Well, he could watch that.

With the subtlety which had kept him for fifteen years in his precarious eminence, he reflected that the fact of Baratá making proposals of any kind might assist him in finding a fair-sounding pretext for sudden war. It would be simple to reject proposals as inadequate, and the mere fact of their being made was admission of an existing wrong. Baratá was assisting him to lead up to a crisis which he had supposed he must be single to engineer.

He considered, in the next second, that a peaceful settlement, if it were sufficiently generous, would be far better than war, which he had never desired, and with which it was too great a probability that the United States would interfere. But a genuine settlement would deprive Bioli of its main political interest, apart from himself. He was glad that nine-tenths of his very considerable fortune was in an English bank!

Even in the event of war, there would be the risk that the United States might insist on changes of presidency after it had knocked the heads of the two republics together, and mopped up the mess. He saw that he walked, as he was wont to do, on a narrow plank. But could Baratá be genuine in making any offer which could be acceptable to him? It was hard to think.

But he also saw that, until he had unloaded that cargo which approached him across the seas, there could be nothing but gain for him in peaceful negotiation, even though there should be little sincerity on either side.

"I shall be most happy," he said, "to know what you propose."

With this encouragement, the envoy of Baratá became specific in statement of the concessions which President Cortéz would be willing to make, if he could be assured that an era of friendship would follow. President Gómez listened, and had seldom found the mask of diplomacy so hard to wear.

It was an incredible offer. It was, indeed, incredible to his mind that President Cortéz should offer anything to anybody except through fear, or in the hope of a larger gain, but there was an open-handed bounty here which would have been puzzling had it come from a more generous source. Coming from a stronger to a weaker state it had a miraculous sound, and President Gómez's belief in miracles was not great. Yet if, in fact, it were unbelievably true? And there was some force in Dr. Dalston's argument that there could be no point in his offering that which President Cortéz would decline to ratify! For one bewildered moment he considered the possibility of disposing of that cargo of arms to a bellicose sister republic too far distant to be of any menace to him, and on terms which would improve his personal banking account more substantially than the Bioli treasury. He considered the possibility that President Cortéz might be suffering from some form of dementia, such as will reverse the patient's previous disposition. He had a fear that he himself might be undergoing an attack of delusional insanity. He said that while there would naturally be points of detail which it would be necessary to discuss, and while the matter was too important for him to decide without consulting his responsible ministers, Dr. Dalston could accept his assurance—his speech became florid with expressions of regard for the neighbouring republic, and for the President and Envoy of Baratá.

Enrico said that he would telephone President Cortéz immediately on his return to his own residence, conveying these expressions of high esteem, and indicating that the offer which he had brought had been favourably received.

CHAPTER ELEVEN

JULIANA ENTERS THE FIELD

JULIANA, having ridden until a later hour of the morning than her custom was, must return as the sun gained power in a brazen sky. She met her father as he was retiring for the midday siesta which is the universal custom both of Bioli and Baratá. She was the one person on earth to whom he would speak in a free way, having confidence both in her loyalty and discretion, such as he could not feel for any of the ministers of Bioli, and more respect for her wits than he was himself aware.

"The question is," he said, "is he sincere, or has he come here to dupe us with lying words? If you can tell me that, I shall find it simpler to deal with this offer in the right way."

Juliana had persuaded herself that she was in some doubt of Enrico's good faith on other grounds, but she found that she disliked the suggestion when it came from her father's lips.

"He is sincere," she said. "He would not lend himself to Baratá's tricks. I should have thought you could see that."

"So he may be. But are they?"

"Can you not judge that by whether the negotiations are dallied or hurried on?"

"We may judge that, if they lag, they are not honestly meant. But, if they are hurried on, how can we tell that what is given now will not be taken back at a better time? They may make us dance to another tune when they have armed themselves to be stronger than they are now."

"Well, I will find out what I can."

"I should be glad if you lose no time."

Juliana stood in a frowning doubt, swinging the broad-brimmed hat which her complexion required when she rode in Bioli's sun. She bit her lip, as she had done when they had talked of Dr. Dalston before. But after that a smile dimpled an olive cheek.

"Did he ask for me?"

"He seemed annoyed that you were not here."

"So he was intended to be. Well, I will see what I can do."

She spoke now in a confident tone, and, as she walked away to her own room, the smile did not leave her lips. It might be judged that she took some pleasure in her own thoughts, though with less certainty that Enrico Dalston would find that they portended pleasure for him.

However, he was pleased enough when he heard her voice on the telephone as the afternoon cooled, inviting him, with the freedom of her English education rather than in accordance with the custom of Bioli, to come over to the Presidency for informal renewal of the acquaintance which had been interrupted so few days before. Tomorrow, she said, there would be a formal reception in his honour, as the new envoy of Barátá; but tonight it would be a quieter opportunity for her to hear the exciting experiences he must have had.

Her tone as she said this was light, casual, and yet with a tone of intimacy and even eagerness to learn of the events which had brought him to so unexpected an official position. But it was on a basis of friendly feminine interest, such as will make trivialities its concern, rather than as touching on more important issues. Naturally, he said he would come.

He found himself received with a friendliness more in accordance with the expectations he had formed from their previous parting than her own plans of an earlier hour. He dined with her father and herself, and sustained without embarrassment his part in a conversation which both host and hostess directed to European rather than South American topics, political or social, avoiding absolutely the differences between the two republics, or the embassage which he had undertaken.

But at a later hour, when her father, pleading the cares of office, had withdrawn, she turned the conversation, with swift directness, from idle comparison of the South American mate with the tea of the Eastern Hemisphere, to ask: "How on earth did it happen? It must have been all settled in about ten minutes after you got out of the train. I didn't know that you had anything to do with Baratá's politics, or that you knew anyone in the Government there."

"Practically, I didn't. Except for meeting Señor Serati on the boat coming out."

"Yes, of course, that was it!" Her face clouded as she recalled the events of the voyage. How secretly must those negotiations have been conducted, while he had seemed to be idling his time with her! Had he really had political aims, perhaps intrigues, which had been kept in a diplomatic reserve, even while he had appeared to talk in a confidential manner?

Realising something, though not all, of this doubt, in the mind of one with whom he was most anxious to establish a very different feeling, he answered: "Oh, but it can scarcely have had much to do with that. I hardly spoke to him till the last night, and he was rather rude then." He related, in detail, what that conversation had been.

"All the same," she persisted, "it was that meeting which must have put the idea into their heads. You can't guess what a man like Serati's thinking by what he says. I suppose President Cortéz sent for you as soon as you arrived?"

"Yes, he did in a way. I was arrested at the hotel."

"You were *what*?"

Enrico, having gone so far on the path of confidence, saw no objection to, and certainly felt no reluctance in continuing upon it. He told all that had happened without reserve, adding his hope that he might really be the means of establishing friendship between Bioli and Baratá. His eyes, as he said it, gave a personal application to this very proper sentiment, as though the closer union of the two republics might be typified in that of a President's daughter of Bioli and an envoy of Baratá. But Juliana's wits were at work too busily now to be turned aside for a game which might be played in an idler hour.

"You didn't give them any money?" she asked. "They didn't arrest you for that?"

"No. Nothing of the kind was even mentioned. And as it appears that they knew that I am a fairly rich man, I think we must exonerate them from a suspicion which, I must confess, had been at one time in my mind."

"Yes," she agreed dubiously. "If exonerate's the right word to use. They were just playing a different game."

"You don't seem to have a very high opinion of the Government of Baratá."

"And I shouldn't say it to you?"

"I don't mind what you say to me."

She became briefly silent, a slender, snake-skin shoe drawing patterns upon the polished floor. She looked at him with a straight gaze of eyes which he thought the most beautiful in the world, and which cooler judgment would have found it easy to praise. "Are we talking as friends, or are you the envoy of Baratá?"

"I hope the two may not be incompatible words."

"I wish I could be equally sure."

"It is to make that certain that I am here."

"All the same, you have not answered my question."

"We are talking as friends, which I am sure we shall always be."

Juliana became silent again. If she had had an impulse to express her opinion of President Cortéz or his colleagues, she may have seen that she could give the warning at which she aimed in a more impersonal way.

"You have come to a world," she said, "which you think you know."

"It is strange, of course. But I have always thought of it as my mother's land."

"So it may be. And so, for that matter, it is mine. But I have lived here much more than you."

"And you think my ignorance may lead me into snares which your feet would miss?"

"Did you think that I meant that? You must have thought me a conceited girl! But it is never a disadvantage to know."

"If you tell me, I shall."

"It is a very beautiful land. So you will have seen. So are snakes. They have a beauty which I am fascinated to watch. I think I would much rather be crushed by a snake than torn by a puma's claws. I do not mean that our people are snakes, but they have different outlooks—different ideals—from those which Europe allows. They think different thoughts. I don't feel the same, but I suppose I am sufficiently near them to understand.

"If I were sufficiently roused, I dare say it would come out in surprising ways. I never felt inclined to stick a knife into anyone, but my grandmother did that to a woman who tried to take her husband from her, and if I were sufficiently jealous, I dare say I should think as little of it as an Englishman does of killing a pig. It's in things like that that race tells, whatever education may do."

"If you loved anyone," Enrico replied, with admirable adroitness, to this candid confession, "and he hadn't the sense to know when he was well off, I should say he couldn't get more than he deserved for being such an absolute fool."

"Well," she said, her eyes shining with pleasure at the evident sincerity of this compliment, when she might have heard a more dubious reply, "you couldn't have said anything much nicer than that! But don't you see that you've just proved what I say? You couldn't have said it just as you did if your mother hadn't been one of us. And you're a hundred times more English than I."

"I don't want you to be different from what you are."

"That's very kind of you again, but I wasn't really trying to lead the conversation that way. I was saying how different our people are from what you've been used to in what I expect you still call 'at home,' when you're not reminding yourself that you mean it to be here in future.

"I like our people, with all their faults, because I understand, even if I don't always share them. But there are bad and good, of all characters, in England as well as here, and our bad men are different from anything you've been taught to expect.

"They might shoot at you twice a year, and if they miss—which they're most likely to do—they'll be as good friends as ever between times and expect you to be the same. Perhaps it is that they think courtesy's more important, and life less so, than an Englishman does."

He answered easily in reply to this description of the volatile populations of Bioli and Baratá: "If they can't aim straight, I don't see that it makes much difference whether they fire at you or not—or, at least, not to the one they're trying to hit. It may be rather more serious for someone else twenty yards away, but perhaps that's equally unimportant to them."

"Everything's unimportant when they get excited, except the one thing about which they happen to lose their heads. It's a matter of what they call brainstorm when they're trying to get a European criminal clear of the law. And when it's over, they just cool down and mop up the blood. "

"Well, I don't see why they should have any reason to mop up mine."

He still answered with a good humour he did not entirely feel. He understood that he was being lectured for his own good, and warned of dangers which his ignorance might otherwise fail to see. He was already too much aware of his inexperience not to realise that there was probable cause for a warning which could not be meant in other than a friendly way. But it shook a confidence in himself which was already insecurely based rather upon the sanguine spirit of youth and health than a rational foundation. He saw, in the very ambiguity of her warning, that she did not regard him as having returned to Bioli in a position of added dignity and importance, as he would have liked her to do, but rather as one, perhaps tool or victim, who was exploited by more astute and less scrupulous men.

There was too much probability in this supposition for him to regard it with ease of mind, and it is to the credit of what he actually was that he took her warning in the right way, and was yet able to maintain the integrity of his official position, as, to hold it, his own honour required him to do.

"You think," he asked, giving her words an implication at once wider and more exact than they literally held, "that I am being made the cat's-paw of cleverer men who will get rid of me without difficulty when my use is done?"

"I didn't say that, and I don't know. We should like to think you have brought a genuine proposal for settling the quarrel between Baratá and ourselves; but, speaking as private friends, as we have agreed to do, it's very hard to believe. Nor can we understand why they should have asked you to undertake the negotiation."

"May they not have thought that you would have more confidence in me, as, in a sense, an outsider, than in one of themselves?"

"They may have thought anything. I can't even guess. But they must have known that questions such as tariff revision could be dealt with more readily by those already familiar with the details involved."

"I am quite aware of my inadequacy on the technical side, but so evidently is President Cortéz also, for—as I would have mentioned to your father at dinner had I not thought the occasion unsuitable—when I reported to him by telephone this morning that my proposals were likely to be favourably received, he replied that a deputation for my assistance would leave at once, which will, I understood, arrive within the next forty-eight hours."

Juliana confessed surprise at this information. It certainly looked as though, from whatever motive, President Cortéz was genuinely anxious to find a basis of peaceful settlement before the *Billy Winch* should arrive. Was it possible that he was animated by no subtler or more sinister motive than a prudent fear of what Bioli might do when it had those deadly munitions in its hands? If so, they would have served their purpose without the risk and wastage involved in putting them to their purposed use! It was rather with the object of obtaining as much detailed information as possible to report to her father, than from any more lively interest, that she went on to ask: "Did he say who the deputation will be?"

"I understood that Señor Serati is likely to come, with the late envoy, Señor Philipo, and a Señor Conradi, of whom you may know more than I."

"I'm afraid I don't, though I expect my father will. But weren't you appointed because Señor Philipo had fallen ill? He seems to have made a very speedy recovery!"

"I understood that while his condition of health renders him unequal to undertaking the full duties of the legation, he is anxious to be of any assistance he can in an advisory capacity, at a moment of such auspicious importance."

"He must be quite a patriot! I hadn't observed that his previous duties were particularly exhausting. But you'll be able to judge of that. Perhaps I've said more than enough about matters I don't properly understand, and a lot more than I should if I hadn't felt that you belong as much to us as to Baratá; but I'll just add this to finish, that you can trust my father, if President Cortéz really means to give us a fair deal, that he'll be ready to do the same."

It was an assertion which some of those who had done business with Bioli's President might have hesitated to support, but it may still have been true, and Enrico, saying he believed it fully, spoke no more than he meant. His trouble was nearer home. As may often happen on such occasions, the conversation had influenced both their minds in contrary directions. Juliana, though still profoundly distrustful of anything which President Cortéz might say or do, and regarding the appointment of Dr. Dalston to his present office as a puzzle beyond solution, had yet come to recognise the possibility, however slight, that the overtures he brought might be honestly meant; while he, from bright vague dreams of becoming the benefactor of a continent brought to federated friendship by his own skilful diplomacy, had come to an apprehension, more immediate, though equally vague, that he was no more than the simple pawn of a drama he was neither desired nor expected to understand.

"It is a queer business," he thought, as he drove home through broad white streets black-shadowed beneath the light of the tropic moon, "and I should have been wiser to decline an office which could hardly have been thrust upon me without more reason than I can see." He resolved to be very watchful, very wary in all he did. Yet what was there to fear? He had undertaken a mission of peace, which, at the worst, could deserve no blame. Should he fail, things would be no worse than before.

And, after all, need they fail? He thought, with some renewal of confidence, of the wealth which was his in another world. With sufficient cause, he might tip the scale with a golden weight, and he was well aware of how potent is the argument of gold in these Latin lands.

Besides, could he be impatient of that which had brought him back to Juliana's side? Which had led her to reveal an interest in himself which he believed to be of a personal rather than a political character? Perhaps he would never give adequate heed to the peril in which he stood, or the falsehoods of those among whom he moved, so long as there would be truth on a girl's lips. And if that were so, there was the greater need for her to be watchful on his behalf, if his life had value to her. But how can even the sharp eyes of love, the keenness of feminine intuition, watch against a danger of which they have no knowledge, and which it would be fantastic to presume?

Now he put intangible apprehension aside, that his mind might be clear to recall the kindness which he supposed he had seen in a woman's eyes, and meanwhile Juliana was saying of him: "He is sincere enough. I can promise that. But he is simple in the English way. He believed all that President Cortéz said, even when it sounded absurd, and he was as ready to believe me, although I am, as you might say, on the other side."

Her father asked, in a tone which might have been more anxious had he known his daughter less well than he did: "You were careful in what you said? It would not do for him to report anything to Cortéz which could be made cause of offence."

"Yes, of course. I only talked in a general way." She went on to the tale of Enrico's arrest, and the events that followed, as she had had them from him, which did nothing to simplify the affair in President Gómez's mind.

At the same hour, Enrico was the subject of a conversation in Baratá which was of more moment to him.

President Cortéz sat with his Minister of Health on his palace balcony, drinking together in the pleasant coolness the night-breeze brings. The swift tropic sunset was two hours gone, but the moon gave light enough for the occasions they had. It would, indeed, have been sufficient for the reading of a small-print book, but President Cortéz did not require it for that. He thought that the brief hours of life could be used in much better ways.

"I have instructed Conradi," he said, "who, as you know, is accustomed to act alone. If you make no mention of the subject to him, he will say nothing to you. You will know next of a thing done, at which you will be properly shocked. It will be evident that such a crime could only have sprung from the evil minds of those who are already importing arms to make attack on a peaceful state, which desires friendship with them; and that it will be intended to make our advances of no effect, as of course, it will.

"You will return at once, but I can leave all detail to you, knowing that you will act as a man surprised."

"It is a bomb he will use?"

"I have left all details to him. It is the better the less we know. But I may tell you that. Yes, he will proceed in the way which is familiar to him."

"They will not be able to prove that it has been manufactured here?"

"Is Conradi a child? It will be provable, if the fragments are kept, that it is of Bioli's making. And, indeed, why should we assassinate our own envoy? It would be absurd to suppose."

Señor Serati fell into the silence of a man who has that on his mind which he must ponder before he speaks. When at last he did so, it was to ask no more than: "You are sure that it is the best plan?"

"If you have another?"

"It came to my mind that Philipo will be there, and that he might be the better choice. That for which he was reluctant to volunteer might yet be an honour he should not miss."

"Why should we alter a plan which is smoothly made?"

"I do not say that we should. I only thought that Dalston is of English birth. May there be no complication in that?"

"None that we may not turn to our own gain. You will suppose that I have considered this. But the assassination of an ex-envoy is not the same thing as that of an envoy, and we could not protest with so loud a voice. It is not Señor Philipo or Doctor Dalston the bomb will scatter about. It must be the Envoy of Baratá."

Señor Serati listened to the President's wisdom, and said no more, though he thought it rather a pity that Señor Philipo might not be so conveniently removed from the little circle of those who farmed the taxes of Baratá. Seeing that he accepted the argument, President Cortéz went on: "In fact, I resolved that you and he should be the ones to go because you will be aware what to expect, and will be prudent not to keep too close to Doctor Dalston's side. I have already told Philipo that Conradi will act at the first favourable opportunity which may occur, or which he may be cunning to engineer, and I have warned him to keep to your side, and to leave Doctor Dalston some space away, so you will see that it is well that there should be no ambiguity about the one on whom his attention will be directed."

Señor Serati saw that without difficulty. The conversation went on to discuss the organisation of the war which was to follow the assassination, and to be carried to Bioli's capital city before use could be made of the cargo upon the seas.

CHAPTER TWELVE

THE STAGE FOR ASSASSINATION

ENRICO waked as the sun rose. He lay in the room which had once been Señor Philipo's, as it was surely his right to do, and it was the best in the house, as it was likely to be. It had a stone balcony outside its green-latticed, wide-opening windows, with a magnificent view over the city, and beyond that to a vista of narrow luxuriant cultivated valleys, and bare, sun-scorched heights, with outlines jagged and sharp against the sky of a lucent dawn.

More to southward, the land fell away to the river gorge, showing a tumble of yellow rocks and wide-stretched forests of glossy green.

Enrico, yawning, looked out on the rising dawn. He said: "No, I'll be damned if I will," with irritation in his voice, which yet had a note of decision which would not be easy to change.

He was thinking of a conversation he had had with Señor Hernández, the First Secretary of the Legation, on the previous afternoon, when he had informed him that Señor Philipo and his illustrious colleagues were coming to San Sebastián.

There were two secretaries to the Legation, but the second was no more than a junior clerk. Hernández was much more than that. How much more was not easy for Enrico to judge. He was a man of mixed Spanish-Indian descent, as were a large proportion of the population of Baratá, to which he, of course, belonged, but his features showed little trace of his European blood. They were heavy and stolid, though there was no lack of intelligence in the sombre eyes.

He had taken Enrico's appearance, and the information that he had succeeded Señor Philipo, in an expressionless manner, giving no indication that he had any feelings regarding it, one way or other. Enrico was soon able to judge that the routine work of the Legation had been left, with little oversight, to this man, as it would still be, for he had enough to do to hide or overcome his inexperience in regard to matters he could not avoid.

But when Hernández had been told that Señors Philipo, Serati, and Conradi were coming to San Sebastián, and Enrico had added: "I do not know whether we should find room for them here, or they will prefer more space in an hotel," he had replied, as one who mentions that which is not in doubt: "Oh, they will stay here."

"Is there room for all?" Enrico asked.

"Yes, there is room enough."

The man added, after a pause, as though it were a relevant consideration: "I do not know who Señor Conradi may be."

"He is, it is most probable, an expert on customs and harbour dues."

"Excellency, he is not that. He can be no more than a clerk. If he were, I should know his name." The man did not speak as one who argues, nor had his words the sound of contradiction, which might have been unmannerly from one in his position. His tone was that of one who does not assert, but merely mentions impregnable fact. After a pause, as Enrico said nothing further respecting the status of the unknown Conradi, he added: "It will be necessary that I find you another room."

He spoke again as one who merely mentions an obvious fact, which it can scarcely be rudeness to do, and Enrico, puzzled for a moment, had replied: "Why should you say that? I am content with the one I have."

"Excellency, it is Señor Philipo's room."

Against the finality of this statement, he had made no immediate reply. He did not wish to act with discourtesy to the man whose office he had succeeded. There might be other rooms in the house equally good, and, put in the right way, it might be an exchange that he would be willing to make. But the conversation with Juliana had nursed a doubt which was already alive. Did Hernández assume that, if Señor Philipo should appear; the new envoy would become subordinate to him?

It was a possibility which had become intolerable to contemplate. He was in a position he had not sought, acting for those whom he did not trust, and if his authority in his own official residence were to be set aside, it would become an office which his dignity, apart from more vital considerations, would not allow him to hold for a single hour.

In this mood, the question of the room became symbolic, an issue, innocent in itself, by which he might resolve whether he were the representative of President Cortéz in Bioli, empowered by him to negotiate a lasting treaty of peace, or the mere tool of an intrigue which he had no reason to trust.

Yet he resolved that he would not act without deliberation, testing each step that he took. He therefore brought the subject up with Hernández, summoning him as soon as he had finished breakfast in the solitude which his official position required.

"Hernández," he said, "you suggested yesterday that I should change my bedroom to oblige what you supposed would be Señor Philipo's desire. I will be shown what other rooms there are."

It was a requirement at which the man showed no surprise, as he scarcely could, for, by diplomatic usage, the house and all it held constituted the private residence of the envoy, though it might be the property of the Government of Baratá.

Hernández did not call a house-servant, as he might have done. He led the way in his impassive manner from room to room showing what choice there was. There were two vacant which were good enough, and a small one besides, but none of them was of the size of the one Enrico was asked to leave, nor were they furnished in equal style.

When he had seen them, he said: "They are good enough, but they are not suitable for the Envoy of Baratá. I will keep the one that I have."

The man stood silent. It seemed that there was even a shadow of obstinacy on the expressionless face, so that Enrico wondered whether he were to be faced by the absurdity of being defied on such a point by his own staff, but when the man spoke at last, he only asked: "Excellency, you will make it plain that it is ordered by you?"

"Why should I do that? You will arrange for them to have the best available rooms."

"Excellency, I might be recalled. I am settled here."

There was a faint note of appeal in the impassive voice, and Enrico, hearing it, recognised a point of view he had not thought of before. Hernández held his appointment, not from him, but from the Government of Baratá. A word from Señor Philipo might be enough to secure his removal to another post, or perhaps his dismissal from the service. So, in theory, might an adverse report from himself, as Hernández's immediate chief. But that was much less than sure. Evidently, the Secretary's judgment was that Señor Philipo had the more formidable power. Probably he was right in that. It was another indication of how temporary, how unreal, was the position into which he had been so suddenly introduced. To Hernández, as to Juliana, it had no appearance of natural stability, of settled power. It was a second warning to be wary in all he did.

So, like President Gómez, he had become alertly suspicious, conscious of the inexplicable, under circumstances which made the inexplicable the perilous also. The weakness of their positions was that neither had the remotest idea of the nature of the danger their instincts feared. Enrico's doubts led him no farther along the path of safety than a resolution that he would either sustain the dignity of the office which had been thrust upon him, or resign it with such abruptness as might be justified by any slight which he might receive.

Having assured himself that his own room would not be disturbed, he ordered his car and made the formal call upon the President which had become necessary to inform him of the coming of his advisory colleagues. He was received with the expected cordiality, but was not pressed to prolong the interview beyond the point which diplomatic usage required. An unreasonable hope that he might see Juliana on such an occasion met its natural disappointment.

In the evening, he attended the reception which was given in his own honour, and found opportunity to renew acquaintance with many of those who had contributed to make his previous visit to San Sebastián pleasant. He moved in an atmosphere of congratulation. It had already become public knowledge that his mission was one of reconciliation, and that, by his instrumentality, Bioli's grievances were to be remedied without the ordeal of war. His part in the matter, vaguely imagined, was magnified in a score of baseless and contradictory rumours, the most popular and detailed of which was that he had offered Baratá a loan of £3,000,000 from the British Government, on condition that Bioli's grievances should be appeased.

But amid these congratulations, sincere enough except when they came from those—always too numerous in political circles—who had hoped to make personal profit from the confusion of war, he was aware of an atmosphere of bewilderment, expressing itself in more than one instance in open cynicism or incredulity. Well, he told himself, he would not allow this atmosphere of unreality to control his mind. Should he fail, it should be because the force of hostile circumstance was too strong to be overcome, and not because the spirit of defeat had been intruded upon him. And, should he succeed, the greater his triumph would be, by the measure of scepticism or ridicule which was around him now.

So he passed from group to group, learning the alphabet of the diplomatist's art; careful to initiate nothing, and to reply in vaguely optimistic or flattering words to inane compliment, probing query, or ambiguous jest.

Juliana, of course, was there. But he saw little of her, the obligations of his position forbidding any personal preoccupation.

With demure propriety, she gave him a single dance, as the President's daughter might be expected to do. After that, he thought that she was deliberate in keeping apart, though there was friendliness' more than once in a meeting glance.

The next morning, hiring a horse, he rode out at an hour and by a route which he knew to be favoured by her, but good fortune was not his.

As the afternoon heat declined, the presidential train came in from Baratá, and the three ministers of its enterprising government descended, entered the waiting car, and a few minutes later passed into the official immunity of the Legation gates.

The stage was set for the drama of assassination and consequent war which had been conceived, a few days before, in the fertile and unscrupulous mind of the corpulent ruler of Baratá.

CHAPTER THIRTEEN

THE ETHICS OF ASSASSINATION

THE twentieth century is an age of specialisation, in which it is a matter of greater honour and more certain profit to be expert in one occupation than to be merely proficient in ten. Andreas Conradi specialised in the removal of unwanted men. He was not a random or illicit practitioner. He would have refused with indignation to become the hired tool of a private vengeance. He served the orders of the ruler of Baratá, and his conscience slept as easily as does that of an English hangman, who will not concern himself as to the guilt or innocence of those whom his hand destroys, and who, if it were demonstrated beyond denial that one of his last year's sheaf of victims had been an innocent man, would still assert (and surely believe) that he himself had done nothing wrong.

Andreas Conradi removed those whom the President of Baratá designated for death, and if he selected them on inadequate or mistaken grounds, that was a matter for his own good angel to explain away, if he could, at the heavenly doors; it was not a matter to cumber Conradi's confessions, or to interfere with the absolution which was regularly given to one of a blameless life. (In fact, how should he know? Was it reasonably to be expected that the President of the Republic would take him into confidence, as to his good reasons for what he did?) It was Conradi's business to see that his work was expertly done, without needless sacrifice of surrounding life, and, above all, so that no suspicion should reach himself, by which his future usefulness would have become less, and (a risk covered by the liberal fees he received) he might find himself criminally charged, and repudiated by the Government whom he so faithfully served.

The degree of his efficiency may be judged from the fact that he did his quiet daily work in the Customs Office of Baratá without a breath of suspicion being aroused as to his more important services to the State. It was understood that he had a moderate private fortune which enabled him to live more comfortably than his official salary would otherwise have allowed. A quiet, inoffensive, inconspicuous man.

There were infrequent times when President Cortéz would send for him for a private interview. It was understood that the President regarded him as an honest man, where such men were rare, and questioned him as a method of checking the official reports and figures which reached him by more regular channels. That might have made him unpopular had it not been observed that certain irregularities of which he was aware, though he refused to participate in their gleanings, went on unchecked after these interviews. Evidently a discreet, intelligent man. One who knew the virtue of silent lips. One who let live, and whom his comrades should treat in the same way.

Conradi had received instructions on this occasion which he did not like. He saw difficulties in carrying out the President's orders in such a manner that no suspicion should settle at his own door, to which he attached importance on his own account, separate from that of the instructions which he received.

But he did not think of refusal. It was his part to obey. When he had suggested the name of a minor practitioner in his dangerous art, who would have been glad to receive half his usual fee, and President Cortéz had put the proposal curtly aside, the idea of avoiding the commission left his mind, and he addressed it to the contrivance which the occasion required.

Actually, it was simpler than his first thoughts had forecast. The baggage of the Government officials, travelling on business of state, was exempt from Customs examination by the diplomatic usage of the two countries. He carried an empty bombshell (which had been in his possession since he had undertaken some political business of a lively character in Bioli, sixteen years before, and which had been manufactured in that country), together with the ingredients for the explosive he would require (separately innocuous till he should mix them), distributed between his two trunks, the locks of which were unopened until they passed into the protection of the Legation walls.

Dr. Dalston, giving courteous greeting to guests who entered a residence to which his own right was no more than two days old, and observing, with no inward pleasure, that their number would not be three but four—Señor Serati being followed by the inseparable Pedro, half a pace at his left rear—shook hands with the one he did not already know, and thought that, if it would be inaccurate to say he would like him more, he might dislike him less than the other three.

Andreas Conradi was of mongrel descent, which would have been an equally true description of at least ninety-five percent of the citizens both of Bioli and Baratá, but he was exceptional in that his ancestry included a great-grandfather of German wood. It may have been due to that element in his numerous racial ingredients that, though not a large man, he was more squarely formed than were most of the inhabitants of the two republics, and that he had a habit of methodical industry, which was even more unusual among them. His passion for the manufacture and use of lethal explosives might be traced back to the Europe of more southern latitudes, but his capacity for using them with success and secrecy was more probably derived from those ancestors who had been bred in a Lübeck street.

He showed no sign of nervousness, and very little of any other emotion, on being introduced to the man whom it had been plotted that he should assassinate during the week. He looked him straightly in the eyes with an almost friendly regard. Enrico thought that he shook hands with a firmer, more English grip than he had recently been accustomed to feel. He supposed that he might be the one man there who really understood the intricacies of the customs duties which they would have to discuss (as in fact he was), and that there might be more assistance to be had from him than from his colleagues of higher rank—that was if there were to be any sincerity in these negotiations of which he was the nominal head, which he was finding it increasingly hard to think.

Yet he found no reason to resent any lack of consideration from the somewhat uncongenial colleagues who had been thrust upon him. Even the allocation of rooms—on which point it was evident that the First Secretary had foreseen Señor Philipo's feelings correctly—passed off with no more than a flicker of lightning which no thunder followed.

There were suavely determined orders from Señor Philipo on the landing. Humbly explanatory words from the First Secretary. Lower-spoken counsels from Señor Serati, which prevailed in the cause of peace. What he had said was: "Suppose he should be annoyed and resign? You can never tell what these cursed English will do! Where should we be then?"

Where, indeed? The assassination of an ex-envoy who was not even a citizen of Baratá would be an absurd pretext for war, and the attitude of President Cortéz toward those responsible for such a fiasco was easier to imagine than it would be to endure. Señor Philipo reflected that the occasion was brief, as he disappeared through his lowlier door. In two or three days' time—perhaps even less—Dr. Dalston's opportunities of insolence would be for ever gone, and he himself would be returning to Baratá, to come again, if at all, to a conquered land, in which he had President Cortéz's promise that he should hold a more important position than that which he had so lately resigned. It would not be the Legation, but the Palazzo of President Gómez that he would occupy then.

For the moment, he must endure insolence with a silent dignity—or at least no more than a word of sarcasm on the subject of Dr. Dalston. He thanked him, as they sat at dinner, for the comfortable accommodation he had received. English courtesy, he said, was proverbial in inferior lands. Enrico met the remark with a baffling smile. "I fear, "he said, "that it is too little we have, and even that has been learnt from those of more southern blood."

He was as resolved as Señor Philipo, though for a widely different reason, that no legitimate cause of quarrel should come from him.

CHAPTER FOURTEEN

TOO MANY LIES

TRAINED duplicity can do much to obscure truth, causing it to mime in a lie's garb, but even duplicity can defeat itself by its own excess.

Enrico, in the negotiations which were so promptly opened on the next day, had the quality of being sincere (stifling some uneasy doubts) in the purpose of what he did; but he was single in that, and comparison may have made the unreality of the surrounding atmosphere more apparent than it would otherwise have been.

His colleagues were content only to show with all possible speed the generous attitude of Baratá, in a negotiation which was destined to close in a few hours to the noise of a bursting bomb. Had they been met in a spirit more genuine than their own, the verisimilitude of the deadly farce might have been easier to maintain. But President Gómez and his colleagues were watchful to discover the true meaning of this parade of generosity in which they found it hard to believe, rather than concerned to bicker upon the details of that which was being offered to them with so strangely open a hand. Their one clear determination was to avoid any possible occasion of quarrel while the days passed, and the *Billy Winch* wallowed placidly toward them through the calm of the summer seas. It was hard indeed, even to these men, practised as they were in diplomacy of the less reputable kind, to maintain an illusion of reality in discussions throughout which Baratá incredibly gave, and Bioli declined to look the gift-horse in the mouth, except to admire its teeth.

After a day and a half, when the long-drawn courtesies of the second morning session were done, Señor Serati spoke to Conradi apart, with more impatience in his voice than his words held: "We cannot prolong this. How can we discuss at greater length that which we offer to give, and they do nothing but talk with a politeness which leaves all details to us? And, besides, that cursed ship is nearer with every hour. Can you not make an end?"

It seemed at first that Conradi would answer with no more than a cold stare. He disliked Señor Serati, and much more he disliked the imprudence of speech. That very quality would prevent him ever uttering a word of criticism of the President of Baratá, but it did not stifle a private irritation that he should have let either Serati or Philipo into the secret of what he was. Had Señor Serati guessed how much greater pleasure Conradi would have felt in preparing a bomb for him and the ex-envoy than for Dr. Dalston, he might have had an uneasy doubt which was never destined to enter his mind; but Conradi did not consider his personal feelings in such matters. He carried out with exactness the orders which he received.

Now, after a scowling pause, he replied: "Señor, it is worst for me. I have to talk figures to those who know, and who find it hard to believe. But I must choose a safe and opportune time. Would you have it within the Legation walls? Or where we are grouped about? At the Garden, tomorrow evening, I will ask you to be alert."

He turned away, giving Señor Serati no opportunity of reply. And, indeed, there was no more to be said.

The Garden of Many Plants is the only product of Bioli's veneer of civilisation of which it has cause to boast. It contains probably the best collection of tropical and sub-tropical plants and trees that the world has seen collected into one place. It was Conradi himself who had made a suggestion of visiting these gardens in the hearing of the President, who had said: "You will let me know when you propose that, so that our police may secure you the privacy which your Excellencies will prefer." And the time had been agreed for the next afternoon, as the heat declined, Enrico being adroitly drawn into the conversation, as assuming that he would be one of the party, so that courtesy would have made it difficult to decline; this he would otherwise have been likely to do, for it was becoming apparent to all that he sought Juliana in his leisure hours, and a good guess that he was not unwelcome to her.

Actually, she was talking of him while Señor Serati enquired thus of his coming fate. She sat alone with her father at the light meal they would take together before the midday siesta commenced. He had said: "We listen, and we agree, as we are likely to do, for the talk is of gifts to us. But I cannot believe. Nor—and it is this which troubles my mind—can I see what the snare may be."

"Doctor Dalston believes that it is fairly meant; or it will be so far as it rests with him. I am sure of that."

"So I am disposed to think. But I like it no more for that. I have never seen why they made pretext to send him here."

"You think that they aim at it ending in some discredit which is to fall upon him, so that they will be free of blame?"

"It is some plot of that kind, though I cannot see what it can be."

"If he knew, I would find out. But it is not sense that he would. He is coming here later this afternoon."

"Very well, I will make excuse to leave you with him. You must find out what you can."

It was a conversation which left both father and daughter content. Juliana wished to be alone with Enrico, and this idea that she could be used to obtain information of political value from him was most satisfactory in its results; besides that, she was genuinely anxious to help her father in a dilemma the full seriousness of which she did not lack the wit to see.

On his side, while he valued her co-operation highly—which was no more than its worth—her friendship with the wealthy English doctor was not unwelcome to him, or, it is mere justice to observe, he would not have used her in such a way, though his own life, or even fortune (which it might have surprised himself to know that he guarded better, and valued more), had been cast in the doubtful scale.

Juliana was well content that she would be left to talk to Enrico alone, but when she recalled her father's opinion that he was being made a cat's-paw in some manner by which he was to be discredited at last, her thoughts took a more sombre colour. She had come to think of his interests as though they were even more personal to herself than Bioli's welfare. She saw also that if he should have reason to be disgusted with his treatment in the new land to which he had come in a romantic rather than a practical mood, he might leave it abruptly, and it was a possibility she did not like. She resolved that when she saw him there should be much to say, including some plain words, which she knew how to use.

CHAPTER FIFTEEN

A Conversation of Many Consequences

"THE fact is," Juliana said, "we've come to the conclusion—everyone on our side who's in close touch with it—that the offer Baratá's making isn't sincere, although we can't guess what it means that they should make it at all."

"You don't think that I may be playing a double game?"

"No, of course not, or I shouldn't be sitting here. And I certainly shouldn't have said what I just have."

"Well, I know what your opinion's been, more or less, all along; and I wish I could say you're wrong more certainly than I feel able to do. But…"—and his eyes, caressing her bare smooth throat, were more eloquent than his words—"…can't we talk of something more interesting? I get customs duties and tariff rates most of the day."

"There's nothing more interesting to me." Her upward glance softened the abrupt reply, and there was a serious intimacy such as might not have been implied by more amatory words, when she added:

"Enrico, can't you see that I'm afraid they're making a fool of you?"

"And you don't want that to happen?" he asked, with more satisfaction for her solicitude in his voice than fear of the threatened fate.

"You know I don't—for your sake as well as ours."

"Then," he answered seriously, "I don't think you need be afraid."

"But I am. I'm afraid of something—all the more because I can't guess what it is. In this country, it's the things you can't understand that you learn to fear."

"Perhaps," he smiled, "they don't understand me."

"I can't joke about it. It's far too serious."

"I'm not joking. I may have one or two cards to play that they haven't guessed."

"Well," she said doubtfully, "if you feel so sure!"

"I'm not feeling anything one way or other. Not about that. I'm feeling something quite different." She half-lay on the soft couch that she preferred because its yellow silk sustained her exotic beauty of hair and eyes, and he stood over her as he spoke. They both knew very well what was in his mind before he added: "Juliana, what about being kissed?"

She looked up with eyes that invited and yet denied. "You look," she mocked, "like a panther about to spring! But this isn't England, you know. Girls don't allow themselves to be kissed, except by the men they intend to marry, and not often by them."

He remembered a somewhat different account which he had heard from Señor Serati's lips, but it would not have been opportune to quote, even had it come from a better source. "You know," he said, "that is what you are going to do."

"Marry someone who hasn't asked me? It doesn't sound very likely, does it?"

"Juliana, will you marry me?"

"I might. Girls do silly things like that."

It was half an hour later that Juliana, her hands as she spoke bringing some measure of order to a dishevelled head, asked with a gravity in her tone which had been absent during their more recent exchanges: "Don't you think you ought to tell me now what those cards are that you haven't played?"

He thought a moment, searching for anything which, though it might be confided to the girl he loved, might not, consistently with his own honour, be said by the Envoy of Baratá to the daughter of Bioli's President. But he saw no reason for silence. They were no confidences of Baratá which were on his mind.

"You have heard," he asked, "of the *Billy Winch?*"

She found it was she who must reply with a guarded tongue. She knew all about the *Billy Winch*. But how did he? It was not a subject on which to become chatty with the Envoy of Baratá.

"Yes," she said, "I've heard the name. What do you think you know about it?"

"Probably all you know—which I don't ask you to say. And one thing which you almost certainly don't. It's one of our own ships."

"It's one of *what?*" Comprehension came to her puzzled eyes. "You mean it belongs to your own line?"

"Not exactly. Had that been so, our friends in San Cristóval would probably have known it, and I've often wondered whether, in that event, they would have acted just as they did. It belongs to a subsidiary line in which the one of which I am a director has a controlling interest. If I should wireless the captain to return to London, or even to alter his course to Baratá, he would obey my instructions without question."

"You wouldn't do such a thing as that?"

"I shouldn't send the cargo to Baratá."

"Anyway, I should have thought that whoever's chartered the ship—"

"Might have a legal claim for damage under such circumstances? But the captain wouldn't concern himself about that. He takes his instructions from his owners, before anyone else."

"How would he know that the cable really had come from you?"

"There is such a thing as a code."

"It's very interesting—very important, too, I daresay—but I can't see where it leads."

"I'm not sure that I do myself. But let me ask you this: suppose I could offer the Government of Baratá a loan of a quarter of a million pounds, on condition that they should make a real peace with Bioli; what do you suppose its effect would be?"

"Could you really do that?"

"It is not impossible."

"I should say that, for less than that, they would collect their mothers and burn them on the Grande Plaza of San Cristóval."

"Then I think I can promise you that Bioli will get what it wants without unloading the *Billy Winch*."

Saying this, Enrico may have felt that he could expect Juliana to look pleased. It is surely preferable to marry one who can compose the differences of contentious states in so lordly a way, rather than one who is to be the frustrated tool of more cunning or able men. But Juliana did not look pleased. She looked doubtful, puzzled. Indeed, regarding the expression of brows and lips, it would not have been difficult to conclude that there had been disappointment in what she heard, and this deduction would not have been utterly wrong.

The fact was that she had had her own plans further advanced than the proposal of marriage which had come so easily, but, at which, had it been less spontaneously offered, she had resolved to arrive before the evening was through. The young ladies of Bioli may be frugal in their premarital kisses. So she had asserted, and Enrico had accepted her statement without denial, though his opinion of its absolute verity, dubious before, must have suffered further assaults from his experience of the half hour that followed. But, if this proposition be accepted, it is surely a conclusive argument that the marriage of those in the mood to kiss should not be delayed.

So, at least, it had seemed to her, as she had lain awake during the previous night, making bold and very confident plans for securing that which she was resolved that she would not miss.

Enrico might quarrel at any moment with those who, she felt an instinctive certainty, were making him their tool, in some way which she could not guess. He might return to England, in consequence, almost at any hour. There might be developments which would render it the only prudent—the only safe—course to take. She knew the habits of her own land sufficiently to see the probability of that; and she had resolved, with all the coolness of her European education, and all the heat of her tropic blood, that he should not do so alone.

Her programme for the evening had been: a proposal of marriage, an urgent expression of her fear for the safety of her accepted lover, finally, suggestion of a secret and instant ceremony, so that she could leave with him at any subsequent moment, if it should become prudent to go.

It would have been hard for her to say how far this idea was prompted by genuine fear that she might lose him should she delay, and how far it had found hospitality in her mind because it gave excuse for that which it would be pleasant to do. But as he showed her a different possibility, foreshadowing triumph rather than flight, her first feeling was a disappointment which was no less sharp because her reason saw that it might succeed. Indeed, her reason found itself, as will often be the issue of such differences, called upon to support her feelings, even though it might not be an easy task. But it showed some obedient ingenuity in an occupation at which it may have had practice before.

"I don't like it," she said, "about you stopping the *Billy Winch*."

"I didn't say that I should."

"But you said you might. I'm certain my father would never forgive that. He's set his heart on those guns, or whatever they are. He wouldn't think any the better of it because you lent a lot of money to Baratá."

"But if the effect of that loan were to be that he got the customs revision which all the fuss is about?"

"Even then, he wouldn't like not getting the arms, and I don't see...."

She checked herself abruptly, observing the danger that he might give way to her protest, which would leave her foiled and weaponless once again. In fact, he had not said that he would divert the ship from Bioli. He had only mentioned the power which lay in his hands, through his being able to do it. Probably the necessity would not arise. Rather, its importance might cease, and it might become an unwanted nuisance, for such disposal as ingenuity could suggest. In ten seconds he might have pledged himself to do nothing without her father's consent, and where would she be then?

She changed the subject with baffling abruptness, to ask: "When you talked about marrying me, I suppose you really meant what you said?"

The query, thrust so abruptly into what had had the sound of serious difference a moment before, might have been taken as a threat of breaking the hour-old pledge should she fail to get her way in this first contest of wills, but so sinister a meaning was denied by the half-challenging, half-mocking, and wholly inviting glance with which she interpolated it into her own half-spoken argument.

Enrico may be excused some bewilderment, but it was a question which admitted of only one reply. "You know quite well I meant what I said."

He would have supplemented his words by an emphatic embrace, such as she had experienced before this last conversation began, but she eluded it with a quick twist and hands which held him back with more strength than he would have supposed her to have.

"But you meant to put it off as long as you could?"

"I wouldn't put it off for an hour, if I had my way. It would be tomorrow, if it could be arranged."

She considered this with a demure gravity, as though it were a new idea, seriously proposed.

"Do you think the afternoon would be a bad time?"

"Any time would be good to me."

"I meant because it's so hot in the afternoon."

"Well, that's for you to say. If you really mean—"

She still held him back, though with a difficulty which did not decrease. "The point is," she said, "that it's a time when everyone else would be asleep."

He saw her meaning clearly now, though its implications were not easy to understand. He had not supposed that, if he had her own consent, there would be further difficulty to be overcome. He wanted her for herself, as he would have done had she been the daughter of the poorest labourer in Bioli, or even of Señor Serati, which is saying a good deal more; but he had supposed it to be a union which could be openly announced, and which her father would not disapprove, but which would only be consummated with some delay, some formality, and the display which so many women desire. But it was a matter on which she must have her way, and she was the more likely to estimate its difficulties accurately. Certainly, if her judgment or inclination favoured so instant a ceremony, he would not be the one to make difficulty, be it public or done in a secret way, even though he might not appreciate the reasons which seemed real to her.

"You mean," he asked, "that we're to manage it without President Gómez knowing?"

"I mean that if he knows, he'll want it to be a formal affair, probably in three or four months' time, and if you're going to queer the pitch about that cargo in the meantime, it's about ten to one it wouldn't happen at all."

"But—," he began, and then stopped, as she had done on the threshold of the same doubt. How he congratulated himself that he had not been more hasty of speech three minutes earlier! He had had no intention of interfering with the voyage of the *Billy Winch* in any way which President Gómez would not approve, and had no doubt that he could have reassured her on that point beyond further question. But as she took it the way she did, was it for him to persuade her to a different mood? It would have been a morality unrecognised in the courts of Love!

His mind turned eagerly to confront the practical difficulties of the proposal with which he recognised himself, from ignorance of Bioli's customs and laws, to be ill equipped to deal.

"You think," he asked, "that we shall be unobserved in the afternoon?"

"Have you ever seen San Sebastián at two P.M.? It isn't likely you have! English though you are, you've probably been asleep too. But I did once. There was a cart here and there, with the driver lying by it on the side where the shadow would come, and the horse's head hanging so that you could see it was asleep too. There wasn't a dog that you could have waked with the first kick. I tell you *nobody's* awake here at two in the afternoon. Two A.M. would be a different matter. I don't say no one would see us then."

"It seems a sound proposition when you put it like that. Anyway, you can be sure I shall be—wherever you say it is. And I suppose you'll get someone to stay awake to perform the ceremony?"

"Yes. There'll be no difficulty. Father Antonio at the Cathedral wouldn't refuse me a little thing like that. Anyhow, he's never refused me anything yet. Even one or two absolutions I haven't really deserved."

"Are there any formalities that I ought to attend to before then?"

"Not that I know of. This is a religious country. It's quite different from our European ideas. If you're married properly in a church—well, you *are* married, and the State couldn't alter that if it tried. And if you're not married in church, well, you're not, and that's the end of that too. But, anyway, you can trust Father Antonio to see that I'm too much married for you to get rid of me in an easy way."

"Then I'm to leave all the arranging to you?"

"Yes. It will be a lot safer than butting in. As a matter of fact, I'm going to confession now, or at least as soon as you'll have the good manners to go, and I don't suppose there'll be much left to arrange when I'm through with that."

Having received so plain a hint, and with the knowledge that Juliana would be so admirably occupied after he had gone, Enrico could not delay his departure indefinitely, and it was scarcely more than half an hour later that he drove back to the Legation, with the memory of a girl's kisses intoxicating his mind, and the knowledge that he was to meet her next at the Cathedral, in the Chapel of St. Gregory, at two P.M. on the following day.

He slept well, having a very happy and confident mind, as was natural to health and youth, and the expectation of such a bride on the next day. He was undisturbed by that which he did not know. But Andreas Conradi, in the privacy of his locked room, prepared a bomb which was not likely to fail, and Señor Serati, propped with many pillows, and smoking the cigar with which he was accustomed to dose the activities of the day, let a crime novel fall from his hand, as he rehearsed the eloquent and manly protest which it would be his duty to make when the Envoy of Baratá should be shamefully assassinated by those whom he had sought to befriend.

CHAPTER SIXTEEN

AN OBSERVATION OF THE COMING STORM

PRESIDENT GÓMEZ, though having a firm confidence in his daughter's discretion, had been somewhat perturbed by the lateness of the hour at which she had dismissed Dr. Dalston from the drawing-room which he had deserted to them.

Hearing the sound of the Envoy's departure, he lost no time in seeking the girl whose bright eyes and somewhat heightened colour suggested that, whatever secrets of state she might have learned for her country's good, the process had not been without some excitement for her of a pleasant kind.

"I hope," her father said, somewhat dryly, "that you have not talked so long without having some profit to show. You should have learnt much in the time you have sat here."

"So I have," she replied, with a demeanour which seemed too gay for so grave a theme; "when you hear what it is, you may think that Bioli's troubles are done."

Her foot tapped a dance-tune on the floor as she stood, in some haste to be gone, yet seeing that there was more which must be said first, though she thought he saw a way by which it need not be much. ("What it is," he thought, "to be young! Do they never tire?") "I have found," he said, "that when Bioli's troubles are less, those of her President will change in an opposite way. But if you have learnt something of moment, I shall be interested to hear."

"I think," she said, "that Doctor Dalston may prefer to tell you himself. But you know that he is a wealthy man. I believe he would spend largely before he would fail."

President Gómez considered this with gravity. He did not doubt that bribery would do much, but he did not think Enrico Dalston to be one who would be likely to employ it, at least, not in its cruder forms. "Well," he said, "money is a great power. Is that all you can say?"

"I will tell you more tomorrow," she answered, "if Enrico does not. But I am really in a hurry now. I have to go to confession to-night."

"At this hour?" He had noticed her unconscious use of Dr. Dalston's Christian name. A thought hesitated at the threshold of his mind that she might have something to confess of which she must discharge her conscience before sleep would come—something which had not been on it even a few hours before. Such are the suspicions of Latin lands!

"Have you so much to confess," he asked, "that it will not wait?"

"Oh, no," she said lightly, "I shall have the usual trouble to make a tale. If you had taught me some of the major sins! But I told Father Antonio that I should be there, and he will be too likely to wait."

President Gómez did not dispute this probability, nor did he make any effort to detain his daughter further.

The Cathedral was not more than a quarter of a mile away, and Juliana would have enjoyed the walk in the cooler atmosphere of the early night; but it would have been a breach of Bioli conventions for any woman of respectable character to walk the streets unescorted at such an hour. Having planned so much more serious an escapade for the next day, it would have been folly indeed to draw earlier eyes upon what she did. She ordered her own car, which had already been warned to be in readiness, and drove to the fulfilment of the obligations her creed required. The chauffeur, who had expected to wait ten or fifteen minutes at the most, found the time lengthen to nearly an hour before she reappeared. But was that any business of his? Could he tell how many sins, or in what detail, a President's daughter must confess? Especially when the confessional is not her most frequent resort.

It seemed, by the lightness of her step as she came out, that the burden of sin must have left her back, however long or difficult the process had been.

She had, in fact, had more opposition than she had expected to meet, but she came away from a struggle which she believed herself to have won.

Father Antonio might be fond of her, but he was not therefore indifferent to the wisdom of what she did, or to the consequences which might come to his own door.

Yet in the end she prevailed so far that she had his promise that if she and Enrico Dalston should be at the Chapel of St. Gregory at two P.M. on the following day, he would be there to unite them according to the solemn rites of the Church, and that he would provide the witnesses which the law required.

After she had left, the old priest considered the matter further in a disturbed mind. The power of President Gómez was great, and, should his anger be stirred, he had shown himself more than once before to be a circumspect and relentless foe. Even the protection of the Church (should it approve Father Antonio's action) might not avail against it. He was an old man, most unwilling to be disturbed from the position of comfort and honour which he now held.

He considered calling upon the President, and only put the idea aside when he reflected that it would be difficult to contrive, within the few intervening hours, without his visit coming to Juliana's ears, which he would prefer to avoid. But he wrote a letter, which he thought that he had so worded that it was not inconsistent with the promise which he had made to her. It said no more than: *"I have been requested by the Señorita Juliana to marry her to Dr. Enrico Dalston, at 2 P.M. this afternoon in the Chapel of St. Gregory, which I have undertaken to do."*

But Juliana had no suspicion of this treachery (as she would have considered it to be), and, like Enrico Dalston, she slept well. She waked to morning skies that were grey with clouds which, at that season, Bioli did not often experience; but she gave no heed to them, having (as she thought) more immediate concerns, and no suspicion of how momentous to her and her lover they were destined to be. Having no thought of bombs threatening Enrico's life during the latter part of the day, her thoughts went on from the marriage ceremony to the night, and to contrive how it could be spent in the manner which brides expect, without premature scandal or exposure of the secret rite of the afternoon. This might be the most difficult part of the enterprise on which she had so resolutely and gaily embarked, for she had said no more than the fact when she had told Enrico that the people of Bioli are more liable to be wakeful at two A.M. than at the same hour of the afternoon.

But she viewed even this contingency with a cheerful and sanguine mind. "If they do," she thought, "it won't matter so much that we need lose any sleep for that. We've only got to explain."

President Gómez got Father Antonio's letter on leaving the Council Room, where he had been receiving the delegation of Baratá during this and previous mornings. The present session had been short, it having been agreed that certain schedules of the revised tariffs should be referred to President Cortéz for the formality of his approval, and that, in the meantime, the conference should stand adjourned.

He was alone when he read the letter. It may be supposed that he felt some surprise, though he showed no outward emotion. He had trained himself not to betray his thoughts by facial expression or gesture, and this restraint persisted, even when he was unobserved. He considered, should he intervene? The time for that would be soon gone. He had no objection to the marriage in itself, or, at least, he would not have had, if it had been proposed in a more open manner. Now he had to consider what the secrecy might imply.

He did not see why Juliana need have feared to ask his consent, and so, with some reason, he was disposed to attribute the method which had been chosen rather to Dr. Dalston than to her own impetuosity, to which it rightly belonged. Unless, of course (he thought), she had been guilty of such indiscretion as rendered a prompt marriage necessary for the maintenance of her own honour, which he was rather reluctant to suppose, and no less so because he had deliberately permitted the occasions from which such follies may be conceived. Putting that possibility aside, he asked himself what Dr. Dalston's motive could be. It was a question not easily answered, unless the Envoy of Baratá foresaw developments which would soon render him unwelcome in such a relationship.

He recalled what Juliana had said the night before about Bioli's troubles being ended by some operation of Dr. Dalston's wealth. He saw that her frankness at that time had been very limited in its range. Yet he felt sure that she had been sincere in what she had said, and he reminded himself that she was not one (unless partiality blinded his eyes) who would be easily fooled; neither did it enter his mind to doubt her loyalty to himself.

He did not suppose that she was making a personal sacrifice in her country's cause. Her attitude last night had not been that of one who sets out on a martyr's path. But she might have the wit to get that which she would for herself, and still contrive that Bioli should gain. If he were to interpose now, through distrust either of Dr. Dalston or her, he might do harm rather than good at a critical moment, and this risk was no less because he would be interfering in that which he did not understand. A habit of caution, which had learnt to tread slowly on unsure ground, inclined him to avoid interference now. He saw that if he did nothing, he would have a knowledge of the marriage which might be shared by none other than the two most immediately concerned and those present at the ceremony. He was aware not merely that knowledge is power, but that its power is doubled when it is secretly held. Unsure of the wisdom of what he did, he yet resolved to trust his daughter's judgment and let the marriage proceed in her own way.

He wrote to Father Antonio: "Let it be as the Señorita wills, but see that those present shall speak no word till my time arrive, if they would continue in Bioli."

Having sent this note by a sure hand, he went to his siesta with as much ease of mind as he was accustomed to feel in these days, and, as he did so, he observed that clouds, black and heavy, were moving up from the sea. The heat was even more oppressive than was usual at the noonday hour. "Those who will wed this afternoon," he thought, "must get wet," for he made a correct guess that one, at least, would walk to the Cathedral rather than take her chauffeur into a confidence which might not be kept. He did not foresee a further consequence in the postponement of the visit to the Garden of Many Plants to the next day, nor, had he done so, would he have regarded it as of any importance at all.

CHAPTER SEVENTEEN

OF MARRIAGE, AND ASSASSINATION DEFERRED

"Señor," Hernández said, in reply to Dr. Dalston's query as to the meaning of that black bank of cloud that rose in the eastern sky, "there will be rain in the next hour, or it may be two."

"Rain that will last?"

"It will last till sunset, or through the night. But after that it may be fine again for two weeks or three, for the wet season is not due till the month end."

This was immediately after the delegates had returned to the Legation. The First Secretary explained that which was known to all but Enrico there.

"Then," Enrico said, "it will not be a good day to go to the Garden of Many Plants?"

He suggested that which he would be glad to hear, having a more important matter upon his mind, though he had supposed that there would have been time for both. He would have been startled by the idea that his own life would thereby be prolonged for a day. But he suggested that to which the others could but agree. Admiration of flowers beneath the deluge which threatened to all would have been an obvious lunacy to attempt.

Conradi, accepting fact, was the first to answer, being quicker to speak than his habit was, seeing that it would be well for him to show no eagerness for that which was to end in death from his own hand. It is by such multiplied trifles that suspicion is so repulsed that it never comes to the closeness from which dangers arise. "It would be," he said, "impossible unless the storm take another way, as it is unlikely to do."

Señor Serati agreed. He said the next day would do equally well, and, as it would be courtesy to acquaint the Chief of Police with their change of plans, it might be well to inform him at the same time of the new date which had been agreed.

It came to Enrico's mind, as it had done when the project was first proposed, that President Cortéz's Minister of Health took an interest in the flora of South America beyond anything which his character or conversation proposed, but he did not therefore regard it as a suspicious circumstance. The idea was too remote to rise in an English mind, as that of Enrico's was by training, and by a predominant blood. Certainly, Señor Serati was disposed to fix the expedition definitely for the next day, to which the others quickly concurred, and why should he object? He had a more important matter upon his mind.

He looked at that advancing torrent of storm with something far from the gratitude in his heart which a man should feel who regards the giver of a further day of life which he is sufficiently young to value at a high price. Caring nothing for him, it spread over San Sebastián's skies till it was met by the mountain walls that rose on the city's northeastern side. Then the rain fell. It fell in the torrential downpour that is seldom felt except in the tropic lands. Few men troubled for that. It was, in any case, the hour of the midday rest. It made no more difference than that those who would have slept on the street, or in the shadier side of an adobe wall, must seek shelter, or be better washed than they often were. It had been an approximate certainty before that the streets would be vacant of human life at two P.M.: the certainty had become absolute now.

The hour moved on, and sleep came to those within the Legation walls, as it came elsewhere. They slept no worse for the noises of falling rain and rushing water along the streets, for there was a time of year when it was music they often heard. There was no danger of flood, for the stone gutters were deep and clear, and the drains wide, in anticipation of such descents.

Only Enrico remained awake in his own room, watching the deluge fall. He did not intend that any flood of not more than wadeable depth should hold him back from his appointment that afternoon, but he had a reasonable doubt of whether Juliana would be of a similar mind. He considered telephoning her for the assurance he would have been glad to hear, but he had been told that the service, though nominally continuing during the afternoon, was precarious in its operations, and he had a more serious doubt of whether such a call might not seem to her an invitation to postpone the ceremony. He reflected that she could equally well call him up should she wish to do so, and that, should she be disposed to avoid the storm, it was a course which she would almost certainly take. He knew that his own instrument was connected directly with the exchange, Señor Philipo having preferred to limit those by whom he could be overheard. While that instrument remained silent, he could suppose that her purpose remained unchanged, as he thought it would. He did not judge Juliana to be one who would easily be turned back from any path she had decided to tread.

It was half-past one when the phone rang. He went to it with a muttered "damn," expecting words which he would not hear.

"Is that Doctor Dalston?"

"Yes."

Hearing his voice in reply, she did not trouble to give her own name.

"I thought I'd let you know that we don't often have rain like this. I mean not till several weeks later than it is now."

"It is rather heavy. But I suppose it doesn't interfere with people's plans much at this time of day?"

"No, of course not. They go on just the same."

"Thanks," he said, "I understand." But the words were wasted. He had already heard the click of her receiver upon the hook.

He supposed that he still had ample time, for he had already decided that he would take out one of the cars himself. He did not intend to reach St. Gregory's Chapel dripping like a half-drowned fowl. He went down to the garage, expecting to find it deserted at that hour, and intending to take the smaller of the two cars.

There was an imposing saloon car for official Legation use, and a smaller open four-seater, with a removable hood. He would have preferred the latter, as the less conspicuous vehicle, had the hood been fixed, which it was not, and had he been confident of its stability against such a deluge as it would have to meet. Having no such confidence, he approached the larger vehicle, and found the assistant-chauffeur asleep within it. Catching him unceremoniously by the ankle, he pulled him out.

An angry growl, as the man bumped to wakefulness on the concrete floor, changed to whining excuses as he saw who it was who had caught him where he certainly had no right to be. He said that he lived some streets away, and had been reluctant to face the storm.

Enrico felt some anger, and that it was politic to show more. He called him a lousy dog, and told him to be off at once, or he would not be wanted again. The man ran out into the rain.

The outer gates of the garage were heavy and awkward to open, one of them having a defective hinge. He was fortunately cautious enough to look into the tank of the car, and found it to be almost empty. When he had filled it, he became conscious that his hands were filthy. He could not go like that to take Juliana's in his! He must wait to wash.

When he drove out into the pelting deluge of water that splashed face-high from the pavement on which it beat, his wristwatch told him that it was within one minute of the hour. Drive as hard as he would through the blinding storm, he must be three or four minutes late for an appointment which should have been better kept.

But he reached the Cathedral with no further hindrance, and when he entered its main door a verger, obviously stationed there for the purpose, met and guided him to the little chapel where the ceremony was to be performed.

Juliana was already there. She had walked through the rain. Waterproofs and a heavy hooded cloak had been cast over the rear row of the chapel chairs, and from them a stream of water made a wide pool in the unlevel tessellated pavement. Even these protections had not been sufficient to foil the rain. The left sleeve of the black-and-gold bolero (which she wore over a white satin bodice and skirt, belted broadly in pimento red) clung damply to arm and shoulder. The soaked arm was raised, as she greeted Enrico with a glance of almost nervous self-consciousness, petulantly adjusting the crushed flowers in her hair.

She looked down as she said: "It isn't a wedding-dress. It's just what I happened to have."

He cared nothing for that, as he was almost clumsy enough to say. "It doesn't matter," he began, and changed to: "You look wonderful." She saw that his eyes approved, and would have been startled to realise how little consciousness he had of the clothes she wore. But Father Antonio waited, and this was no time for delay. She was married with his mother's wedding-ring, which it had been his custom to wear. The time during which San Sebastián was held in the bondage of sleep shortened as they were ready to go.

"You need only slip the hood over your head," he said; "I've got the car close up to the steps."

"But I can't come in the car. I must walk back."

"No, you won't," he said, with a note of ownership in his voice which she half resented, and yet thrilled to hear. "Look at your sleeve now. I'm going to drive you back."

"But if we were seen...."

"There's no more probability of that than if you walk. Less, in fact, because you'll be ten minutes earlier. And I'm going to have no mystery about having taken out the car. I don't suppose I could. For one thing, I've left the garage doors wide open to the street. I came out to call on President Gómez, and that's what I'm going to do now."

"You're not intending to tell him?"

"No, not till you wish. I don't see that there'll be much occasion for any secrecy. In fact, I haven't from the first, but I didn't see any reason why I should press that opinion. I thought the idea was too good. But I'll play fair. I'll leave you to tell your father at your own time, or wait till you say I can."

He had helped her to put on the hooded cloak, and drawn her toward the door as this conversation proceeded, and she entered the car without further demur.

"You'd better wait here," she said, when they had entered the palazzo by a side-door to which she led him, and gained the drawing-room without consciousness of having been observed. "I shall come down in a few minutes, and when Father finds you are here, he won't ask how long you have been. He'll suppose you've just come."

It sounded no more than a reasonable presumption; and if Father Antonio's pledge of secrecy, given in the last hour in the names of all concerned (without mention of the important betrayal already made) should be kept, they had some cause to anticipate that their plan, by its own simple audacity, had prevailed.

Now it only remained to make reality of this puzzling farce into which he had been so bewilderingly involved, and he felt little doubt that he would be equal to doing that. He was in the mood to succeed, and call it a little thing. Having won Juliana, it seemed that he stood over a crouching world. He would begin with a straight talk to President Gómez now, and tomorrow the delegates of Baratá would also hear some words of the right kind. It is hard to doubt, having youth, and health, and affluence, and a waiting bride. But meanwhile, behind his locked door, Andreas Conradi unloaded a most ingenious bomb, and put it away until it should be required tomorrow, about that hour.

CHAPTER EIGHTEEN

THE RETICENCE OF PRESIDENT GÓMEZ

JULIANA came back to the drawing-room a few minutes before her father would be likely to arrive, as her promise had been. With watchful ears for a coming step, they found brief time for the first kisses the day had brought, and for whispered words of even more importance to them.

"When shall I see you again?"

"You will remember the door by which I brought you this afternoon?"

"Yes. I could find that."

"In the dark?"

"Yes, I think I could."

"But you must say you are sure! Will you be there at the same hour? I mean at two. In the night."

"Yes. But how shall I find your own room? Where you are?"

"You must not try. It would be far too dangerous if you should be found in the palace alone during the night. I will come down to the door."

"I am not to knock? Just to wait?"

"Yes. Till the door opens, you will do nothing at all. But you need have no doubt of that. I will open at two."

They broke apart with the last words, for which there had been scarcely time, as President Gómez entered the room.

He may have observed that his daughter's colour was somewhat high and her eyes shone. He may even have observed more than that, but he gave no sign.

He showed no more than the proper surprise that the Envoy of Baratá should have paid him this unarranged and informal call. "I shall be most happy," he said, "to listen to anything which you would like me to hear." He suggested that (with Señor Dalston's consent) mate should be served on the patio. "It is cooler there, and the rain does not intrude."

After they had been seated for a time, and the usual afternoon drink had been served, Juliana excused herself.

"It is not I," she said in her demurer manner, "whom Señor Dalston has come to see. I can observe that your talk pauses until I am gone."

She went to her own room. She had missed her usual afternoon rest. She had reasonable anticipations of a disturbed night. She slept while she could, as it was prudence to do, and her dreams were good.

When she had gone, Enrico opened the subject upon his mind.

"I have hoped," he said, "I should say that I still hope—when I accepted an office for which it must be evident that I am unfitted in many ways, that I should be an instrument of a lasting and happy peace."

"As a fact," President Gómez observed, "we were not at war."

The statement was indisputably true, but Enrico felt a rebuff. He recognised that he was expected to expose whatever he might have come to say without certainty that his frankness would be met in a kindred mood.

"No," he said, "but when I was here for the first time, I heard talk from which it seemed that war might be farther away, and not far. I suppose I need not say that what I heard then, when I was receiving hospitality here, was not afterwards mentioned in Baratá."

"You were not long there."

"No. But much can be said in an hour. In fact, they said much to me."

"In a confidence, no doubt, which you must also respect?"

"Yes, unless I should see reason to think that I have been deceived."

"Which you think you have?"

"I have not resigned."

President Gómez had a moment of silence, seeing that he was being paid back in his own coinage of meagre words. But he felt that he could afford to fence better than his opponent, having the secret knowledge of what had occurred during the afternoon. He saw that Enrico had something on his mind which he was determined to say, and he was resolved that it should be said without assistance from him, or an equal exposure of his own thoughts. He saw that, when Enrico pointed out that he had not resigned, he implied that, though he might suspect, he did not certainly know.

"You would tell me," he said, "that you suspect, but you are not sure?"

"No, I would say a quite different thing. I am resolved that what I have undertaken shall be brought to a good end."

"So it would appear that it is likely to be. We have accepted concessions from you of which I will say without reserve that they are from a liberal hand, and they have now been submitted to your President for an approval which, Señor Philipo assured me yesterday, will be quite certainly and most promptly given. There is no more that we ask."

"Then there is nothing that I can usefully say, you being content that all is entirely well?"

"Did I say that? Was it not your own doubt that the offer may not be sincere? And you are the Envoy of Barátá!"

"Pardon me. Did I say that? Did I not say that I am still the Envoy of Barátá? But it is clear that there is a doubt, be it yours or mine. And meanwhile the *Billy Winch* is upon the seas."

President Gómez met this unexpected remark with as blank a face as he would have opposed to his deadliest foe.

"The *Billy Winch*," he asked, "being a ship?"

"Being a ship over which I have some control." This was something which President Gómez had not expected to hear, and which required more consideration than a moment would allow. Yet he thought quickly, as he had learnt on necessary occasions to do, or he would not have been President of Bioli for fifteen years without even a scar on his body where a bullet had entered, or a knife-thrust grazed.

He did not doubt the truth of what he heard. He knew already that Dr. Dalston had inherited control of one of the largest shipping lines in the world. That he could exercise some control of the *Billy Winch* was far more probable than that he should make such an assertion if he had no such power.

If President Cortéz had known of this, it explained much which had been puzzling before. Or did it? Perhaps it would be more exact to say that it changed one enigma for another more puzzling still.

But why did Dr. Dalston tell him this now? Was it friendship or threat? It must not be forgotten that he had married Juliana that afternoon. Had he come to confess a plot in which he was no longer disposed to join?

None of these explanations seemed entirely likely. He recalled what Juliana had said on the previous evening respecting the possibility of Dr. Dalston's wealth being thrown into the scale, and the remark with which he had begun the conversation that his desire had been to become the instrument of a lasting and happy peace.

It was a position in which President Gómez decided that he must not be quick to resent anything which he might hear, though the suggestion that Enrico might have power to turn back (or even divert to his enemies?) the cargo which had been so hardly obtained, and at a cost not lightly to be ignored, was very hard to endure. Yet he must hear all with an open and cautious mind. What he said, after a longer pause than, had he been speaking to one who was not his friend, it might have been prudent to make, was: "You mean that you could turn it back if you would?"

"I did not mean to say that, though it may be true. I simply tell you a fact."

"Which I may suppose that President Cortéz already knows?"

"I cannot say that. He has not heard it from me. If I guess, I should suppose not."

"You are proposing to tell them now?"

So he was. But how had President Gómez guessed that? Enrico perceived that he talked with one of a subtle mind, whose thoughts might go far beyond the range of his spoken word.

"Yes. I have thought of that. But I tell you first. If Barátá's present offers are made through fear, it is a bad basis on which to build. I would remove that, if I could, and substitute a foundation which would be more secure."

"By depriving me of a cargo which would be a menace to them?"

"Not at all. I may tell them, with your approval, that I have power to do even that. But that I should use that power is another matter."

For a brief minute the President became silent again. He considered the fact that Enrico had told this to him, and it had a friendly face. Particularly so if he had told him first, which he was disposed to believe. But it was a bitter thought that Barátá's envoy should have such power. Yet he did not fail to reflect that it might be very difficult to exercise without his consent. He could certainly prevent a cable being despatched to the ship from Bioli's territory. But perhaps Dr. Dalston had already taken precautions against that danger by leaving some delegated authority with an agent in Barátá?

He considered that the risk, unless it were already too late, could be removed by Dr. Dalston's assassination, and he had certainly eliminated others in that manner with less urgent cause, on more than one previous occasion. For a moment, the Envoy of Barátá was in real danger of being doubly condemned to death.

But he reflected that the murder of a representative of a friendly state must have serious political consequences, hard to assess in advance of the event.

From an opposite angle, his anticipations approximated to those which had led President Cortéz to arrange the assassination, and so, quite logically, led him to the opposite conclusion that it might be better to let him live.

He remembered also that Enrico had married his daughter a few hours before. That was a factor of importance in several ways. But had it been no more than a form of life assurance for Enrico, before daring to develop whatever plans he had formed?

He felt that a further talk with Juliana was emphatically indicated, and that, in the meantime, and to Dr. Dalston, he should be frugal of words.

"You will not," he said, "divert the ship, in any event, before we have discussed this matter again?"

"No," Enrico answered readily, "I will promise that. It is not a thing I should be likely to do."

He would have gone on, had he been encouraged to do so, to express his willingness to devote such sums to the development of the sister republics as might prove an attractive alternative to the sanguinary quarrel which had been in Gómez's, and probably in his opponents' minds. But the President changed the subject with some abruptness to ask: "You had not, I trust, been waiting long when I came in?"

"No, not long."

"I am happy that my daughter was able to receive you when you arrived."

The remark was met by a rather awkward silence. Enrico remembered his promise not to disclose, without Juliana's permission, the event of the afternoon. He did not suppose that the President could have any suspicion of what had occurred, but there was a tone beneath the politeness of the words which he did not like, and he saw that, if he were not prepared to lie, it was a dangerous subject of conversation to follow.

Knowing what he did, the President was able to appreciate this reticence with an accuracy which went far to relieve his mind on more important issues. The fact that Enrico showed awkwardness on so small a point was, to a mind expert in judging duplicity in all its forms, an almost conclusive argument that he was not boldly engaged in diplomatic intrigue of a more complex kind. President Gómez had too keen an observation, too fine a judgment of his fellows, to suppose that all men are liars because he himself sometimes neglected to worship Truth.

For a few moments the two men sat in a silence pregnant with many thoughts, while the swift tropic dusk darkened around them, and the vines stirred on the patio's outer wall, accepting the rain. And then Enrico got up to go.

CHAPTER NINETEEN

"FOR ONE NIGHT, OR THE OTHER NIGHT—"

ENRICO, driving back through a torrent which did not cease, may be excused if he felt that he had done enough for one day, not only for himself, but for Bioli and Baratá.

He was less consciously intent than Juliana had been upon preparing himself for the experience of the coming night, for a man naturally conjugates the verb To Have, while To Be will have first place in a woman's mind. But he did propose to himself to get such sleep as will come to one who has an appointment at two A.M. which it is imperative that he shall not miss.

His talk with President Gómez had left a feeling of vague disquiet which he put resolutely aside. He attributed it primarily, with more truth than he was in a position to see, to the fact that he had concealed his marriage to Juliana. He resolved that, before morning came, he would have her promise either to tell her father herself, or permit him to do so. He saw it to be a concealment without reason— without proper excuse; and the more so now that he had disclosed his control over the movements of the *Billy Winch*, and the heavens had neglected to fall.

Tomorrow morning he would talk to Señor Philipo and Serati, using even plainer words than had been appropriate at the interview from which he had just come. He might have been a tool until today—he was not sure—it was a puzzle to which it may have been well for his own peace that he lacked the key—but from now he would take control.

So he thought. But he came on those who wished to talk at a sooner hour. In the Legation lounge he found his three colleagues, and the First Secretary, and Pedro also, to whom Señor Serati was giving some instructions which ceased abruptly as he entered, to their surprise, for the sound of the car's return had been drowned by the falling rain.

They had been perturbed men. Three hours earlier they had been informed that the garage doors stood wide, and the large car was gone.

The head chauffeur could give no explanation. It must have happened while he was asleep, as, during the afternoon, all men have a right to be. But he was sure that the garage doors had been closed, so that they could only be opened from the inside.

The assistant chauffeur, having come back to his duties, gave a severely edited version of what he knew. His Excellency had come into the garage, and sent him home through the storm with an angry word. As he did so, he had had his hand on the door of the car.

What was to be deduced from this? The Envoy of Baratá had taken out the car, driving it himself, which was not his habit. He had taken it at an hour given to sleep, when he could expect it to be unobserved. He had taken it out through an infernal deluge of rain, which, without urgent cause, no sane man would be likely to do. He could not have intended to make a call in the city at that hour, for it would have been a monstrous breach of etiquette to attempt, and who would have been awake to unbar the door?

Weighing these considerations in the shallow shrewdness of their criminal minds, they came to a natural conclusion that their intended victim had become suspicious and fled; they were no more likely to guess that he had gone out to marry Señorita Juliana in the Cathedral during the afternoon than he was to guess that he (but for the rain) was to have been blown apart in the Garden of Many Plants. Missing the true explanation, they adopted the only probable one which remained. When Enrico entered the lounge, they were not only relieved, they were startled men.

Señor Philipo was the first to speak. He asked smoothly: "You are unhurt? We had become anxious, learning that you had gone out in such blinding rain. Indeed, we were discussing whether we should inform the police, but were reluctant to do that which you might not approve."

"No. I should have been annoyed. I have been with President Gómez."

"It must have been urgent business at such an hour."

The words were harmless, but there was a faint note of sarcasm in the tone in which they were said. It was too slight to make offence seem reasonable, too definite not to be understood by a sensitive ear.

"So it was. We were discussing the *Billy Winch*." He had answered on impulse, and from the resolution that there should be plainer words in the future than he had been accustomed to hear. His retort was effectual in that those who heard ceased to doubt that he had really been with the President during the siesta hour. They would have been potent to divert suspicion from Juliana had it previously glanced in her direction, which, perhaps naturally enough, it had not done.

It produced a feeling almost of stupefaction upon the little group who faced him. They left Señor Philipo to carry on the conversation, as he had done from the first.

"You discussed that—without previous consultation with us?"

"I believe I am the accredited envoy to Bioli from Baratá."

"But, Your Excellency," Señor Philipo went on—and there was insult in the slight inflection with which the formal title, unusual in conversation among themselves, was stressed—"was there occasion for your colleagues to be ignored? Would you have us think that you chose such a time for a visit of which we were not expected to know?"

"Señor, if you think that, you will be quite wrong. I propose to confer with you tomorrow morning, telling you what I have said to President Gómez, and other things which may be of even more interest to you to hear."

"May we not hear them now?"

"No. For before I put before you certain proposals which are in my mind, I must give them more thought than they have yet had."

It may not have sounded a very convincing reason, but it was better than none. It was well enough. He might, in any case, have been reluctant to enter into a detailed discussion then, but he was the more disinclined because he had perceived an attitude in that little group which the mere fact of his having been out during the afternoon seemed insufficient to explain. There was an atmosphere of latent hostility, against which he instinctively opposed an aloofness of another kind. With the cards he held, he felt that he could afford to speak in his own time, and his own way.

He went out, retiring to his own room, without inviting reply, and he left men who were little less perturbed than they had been before, when they thought him fled. It was their turn to be faced by something they could not read.

Señor Serati was the first to speak, in words which might be ambiguous to a stranger's ears, but were plain to three at least of those who were present there.

"It is possible," he said, "to delay for a day too long."

His eyes were on Conradi as he spoke, making his meaning clearer even than it would otherwise have been. But a whitewashed wall could not be more blank than Conradi's eyes. He thought again that it had been folly to let even Serati know as much as he did. If he were foolish enough to reply, Hernández might guess, if not now, tomorrow when the bomb would burst. He did not doubt the loyalty of the First Secretary, but he knew that there is no silence so sure as that of the man who does not know.

Señor Philipo spoke, with a discreet obliquity, easier for Conradi to admire: "The advantages of avoiding dissension among ourselves are not to be overlooked."

That was a vague-sounding platitude which suggested much more than it said. If there were to be dissension between the Envoy and his brother delegates, and he were to die on the next day, it might at least raise a plausible doubt as to the origin of the assassination on which the Government of Bioli, conscious of its innocence, would be sure to seize. And if he should resign before the event could be conveniently arranged, he would defeat their plans in another way.

It was elementary policy, under whatever provocation, to keep the peace until the next afternoon, even though Dr. Dalston might be committing Baratá to some bargain with President Gómez which they would not seriously approve. Would not all the words of the coming hours be blown away with the smoke of a bursting bomb?

Señor Serati saw all this clearly enough, though the process had taken him some seconds longer than the ex-envoy. He said indifferently: "Well, tomorrow we will hear what he has to say. But there can be nothing further agreed till we have President Cortéz's reply, which cannot arrive before the next day."

A moment later, the little group having broken up, and Señors Serati and Philipo being alone, the ex-envoy said: "Let him propose what he may, we will listen and call it good. It will make no difference at all. But if we should bicker, and he sulk, he might not come out with us in the afternoon, as we require him to do."

"Yes," Señor Serati replied, "we can hear folly and call it sense. We know what Englishmen are. It is the danger that he may bolt that is on my mind. There is more in this than he said to us."

"So I think. But I do not suppose he will do that. He has more affirmative plans."

"Well, it will be no harm if I make sure."

"What do you propose to do?"

"I will put Pedro on guard."

Señor Philipo made no objection to that. He thought it to be of no importance at all, as he did not think that Enrico had any intention of leaving during the night; and if he did—well, who could say whether it would be better or worse that he should find Pedro barring his way?

It followed that, at about half-past one, when the Legation should have been sunk in the heavy sleep that follows the midnight hour, Enrico, opening his door quietly enough, but with little thought that his going would be overheard, almost stumbled upon the body of a man who lay on his back sprawling across the threshold.

Enrico looked down on Señor Serati's secretary or bodyguard, or whatever he might be, in a moment of puzzled doubt. Was the man wounded or dead? Had he been cast there that his death might be literally at his own door? It was evidence of how far his education had proceeded in the ways of these Latin lands that this last possibility should come at once to his mind, and seem a probable thing.

But, as he looked again, with eyes grown more used to a poor light, he decided that the man slept. Whatever explanation there might be of the place where he had chosen to lie and an innocent one was not simple to imagine—it was an occupation which should not be disturbed. Enrico stepped across him with care.

It is probable that Pedro would have had a secret to keep to himself, or the blame of a bad watch, had it not been necessary for Enrico to reach backward across the prostrate form to close the door through which he had come, and as he did so, the motion, or the slight click of the closing latch, disturbed the sleeper. His eyes opened. He was evidently one who could wake quickly at need. For a brief half-second his gaze met that of the man who leant over him. The next, with a movement of surprising lightness for one of his lengthy bulk, he had gained his feet and his wits.

"Excellency," he said, "you will forgive that I was not more quickly alert."

"I shall know better what to forgive when I learn what you were doing here."

"I was placed here for your safety, for which Señor Serati is much concerned."

"Which I am not aware that he has occasion to be."

"Excellency, it is a land in which you have been but a short time. They who hold positions of state are surrounded by many foes."

"Well, I will talk to Señor Serati on this matter. If you had instructions to lie here, I have no quarrel with you. But it is an assistance I do not need. You can go now."

"Excellency, it would be a disobedience I do not dare."

The position was exasperating, and Enrico found difficulty in maintaining the self-control which it required. The appointment he had to keep was not one to be advertised to others, and particularly not to those whom he did not trust; and it was already evident that it must have a partial publicity. He could not hope that his leaving of the Legation during the night would remain unknown, if he should persist in so doing. Yet the thought of Juliana waiting in vain was not to be lightly endured.

He said curtly: "You should know that it is I who give orders here," but he saw no change in the obstinacy of the face which confronted him, unless to a faint sarcasm; which was not certainly to be seen in the dim corridor light. He added: "But if you have orders from Señor Serati to stay here, I will not place you in a position of embarrassment with him. You can do as you were told. Tomorrow I will see that you are better employed."

He turned as he spoke, walking toward the stairs, but the man followed him, even pushing in front, as though he would bar his way.

"Excellency," he said, "I have orders I must observe."

"You may do what you will so that you cease troubling me, which I do not permit."

"Excellency, if you will please to go back to your room now, tomorrow morning Señor Serati can explain, as I cannot do."

"Why! Do you think you can give orders to me?"

The man's eyes shifted before the anger of those they met, but he did not therefore withdraw. They were at the very top of the stairs now, Pedro standing with his back to them, barring Enrico's way.

"Excellency, there can be no occasion to go abroad in the night."

"Am I to judge that, or are you?"

It was a question which Pedro was not destined to answer, for, as it was asked, Enrico's eyes had been on the point of the man's chin, at which he struck an upward blow, driven with the skill of a practised boxer and the strength of his angry determination to clear the way.

It was a kind of attack which Pedro was least prepared to meet, it not being practised in Baratá, but it showed his quickness of eye, and the method of defence that was instinctive to him, that his knife was already bare in his hand as the blow lifted him from his feet and sent him backward into the air.

The flight of stairs was of polished stone, hard and bare. The blow had been delivered with such force that it was twelve steps down that the back of his head struck on a sharp edge, and he pitched, heels over head, down to the stone paving below. Enrico, making a more leisurely descent, could not be surprised that he lay still.

He stood for a long minute in the silent portico, listening for any indication that the sound of the fall had roused the sleepers above.

Maddening though it might be to be thwarted thus, he could not risk that he would be followed to a door which Juliana would open to him during the night. But there came no sign of movement above, and after this watchful pause he let himself out to a silent and empty street.

"Had I missed my blow," he thought, "it might be I who would be lying there, with a knife-wound I should not survive." Life becomes most precious when a desired gift is in its hands, but has not yet been placed in our own. The incident left him with the confidence naturally to be felt by one who, by virtue of his own courage and muscle, has been the victor of such a bout, and yet made thereby sharply conscious of the perils of those who climb to pluck the fruits of life from its highest boughs.

He walked swiftly and lightly, choosing, not without doubt, the shadowed sides of the moon-drenched streets, watchful ever lest a hostile form might leap upon him out of the darkness, and with a thought of regret for the knife which had shone in Pedro's outstretched hand.

But, in any event, he would have had no skill in its use, such as seemed to be the birthright of these people of his mother's land, and his first object now must be, not to win success in another broil, but to reach, unnoticed, undeterred, to that waiting door. He had been reminded that

"One night, or the other night,

Will come the gardener in white,"

but he had a high hope that the night of his coming would not be this.

Let fate be kind till the dawn, and (the lines came to mind, from that acquaintance with the deplorably coherent Victorian poets which was the penalty of his English education)

"Then let come what come may
I shall have had my day."

Or his night, with a more literal accuracy. And this, it seemed, he was not to miss. Through silent streets, he came to a silent door. He was more than a minute late, for the second time that day, but Juliana, waiting behind the door which was opened the inch which invited further pressure upon it, did not observe that in the joy that he had appeared.

Treading softly, and heard by none, she led him to the security of her own room, to know the soft warmth of her passionate arms and other privileges we must not share.

CHAPTER TWENTY

BREAKFAST, AND CONVERSATIONS THEREAT

PRESIDENT GÓMEZ arrived late at the breakfast-table from a wakeful and anxious night, but Juliana was later than he.

"Well," he thought, looking back through the years (for since an older Juliana had died, he had been of a very continent life), "there have been times when I was late for breakfast from the same cause." But as he thought this, his daughter entered the room.

She came radiating youth and health, and the gaiety that is their casual child. She greeted her father as one whose conscience is clear of wrong and who is unaware of any cloud that may darken the coming day.

"I trust," he said, "that you have had a good night."

They were simple words, but as he spoke them their eyes met, and a blush which she could not rule darkened olive cheeks, as her voice, under better control, answered: "Oh, yes. Quite. I always do."

He was silent after that for a time, asking himself how far in denial she would be likely to go, and how far it would be wise to press her to evasion regarding that which (though he had a better hope) she might be resolved that she would not tell.

His eyes watched her hand.

"The ring," he said, "is one that I have not seen."

She raised her bent hand, showing a great Peruvian ruby which had given pleasure to Enrico's mother twenty-five years before it had been slipped on to her own finger, to be admired by the light of the tropic moon.

"I have several," she said easily, "which I seldom wear."

He observed that she was cooler in riposte than she had been at the first exchange, and once more he would not press her to the alternative of confession or utter lie. He tried a more frontal attack, though in a form which she could confound by silence, if so she would.

"It is a custom of most civilised lands to give such rings as evidence of betrothal—or something more."

She looked up at that, so that their eyes met as they had done before, and once more he saw the dark blush which she could not control, but her glance was fearless and unashamed.

"I can see," she said, "that I am to tell—as I promised Enrico that I would—I am to tell you what you already know."

"Did he ask you to promise that? It is good to hear."

Frankness followed, in a conversation from which we may turn aside, as it consisted in exchange of knowledge which is already ours, and conjectures which would have been nearer truth had they included the dominant part in the coming drama which was to be played by Conradi's bomb.

We may turn to another breakfast table, where there is neither beauty nor youth, nor any compensating dignity or fragrance of thought. The three places of Señors Philipo, Serati, and Conradi are filled, but the one at the head of the table, being that of Dr. Dalston, is still vacant.

There is no anxiety over that absence, for they know that the Envoy is in his own room, and will shortly appear. He has already been informed by Hernández of the tragedy of the night, which the three are discussing now. For Pedro, when morning came, was found, dead and stiff, at the foot of the main stairway, having died from a broken skull. He had certainly fallen down the stairs, from which the fatal fracture, and other injuries, any or all, might have come. Or he might have been struck from behind, causing the fall. He had been found with a drawn knife in his stiffened hand, which suggested that he had been aware of the danger he had been unequal to meet.

What had occurred could be no more than a doubtful guess, but his death was not an occasion for deep regret. Indeed, Señor Serati felt a satisfaction he must not show. The man had been useful in many ways. But he had come to know too much. He had become expensive, even troublesome, and the time when it would have become necessary to arrange for his removal could not have been far.

What did matter was that Dr. Dalston was still here. Pedro's death would be of no real importance unless some lying, malicious tale could ultimately turn it into connection with the more important fatality which was to occur in the afternoon, in such a manner as to cast doubt upon the direction from which the bomb had come. That might seem a remote possibility, but these men, having it in their minds to establish a lie, and being confident that the truth could be successfully hidden, knew another lie to be that through which their own would be most vulnerable to attack. They were debating earnestly, not how Pedro had died, but rather what tale should be put abroad, when Enrico entered the room.

He greeted them as a man in good spirits, for which he had more than one reason of which they were not aware. As to Pedro's death, it was to be regretted, of course; but he appeared to regard it as a mystery it was not his business to solve.

"Is it not possible," he asked, "that he may have risen, thinking he heard a noise in the house, and slipped on the stairs in the darkness, as he was about to descend?"

"Which," Señor Philipo answered, "is very much what we have come to conclude, though we agree that it is strange that he should have heard that which left us undisturbed, his room being high up, and farther away."

There was no need to mention now that the man had been sleeping near the head of the stairs, outside Dr. Dalston's room. Indeed, it would be much better that that should not be spoken or guessed, it having become a secret which Pedro could not reveal.

"I had a thought, myself," Dr. Dalston said, "that I heard steps in the night."

"Which," Señor Serati agreed, "may have been his."

"I should have said—though the noise was not much—that there were the steps of two."

This truthful statement was received in silence. No one there, except Enrico, could make more than the vaguest guess as to how Pedro had died, but there was a general feeling that they wanted no complication to arise concerning the manner of that decease. They had a far more important one to arrange. Even if Dr. Dalston knew more than he said (which was not a very probable guess), the last thing they would desire would be to suggest a suspicion of that. Suppose a rumour should get about that the Envoy of Barátá had enemies within the Legation walls? That he had been involved in self-protective violence during the night?

Few things could be worse than that for the purpose they had in view. They were a happy party, animated by common (and generous) aims, engaged upon a mission of peace which would be shattered when the assassins of this wicked, munition-importing State should blow their envoy to bloody fragments in the Garden of Many Plants.

Señor Philipo dismissed the subject of the dead man.

"Well," he said, "he is gone; and with a secret he cannot speak." He went on almost at once—for it had been agreed between the three before Enrico appeared that the conversation which was to follow should be left for his suavity to control—"Señor, you said, last night, that you would have something to tell us regarding President Gómez and the *Billy Winch*."

"Not precisely that. I said I would tell you what I had already had occasion to tell him. That is, that, if I would, I could change the course of the *Billy Winch* to another port."

The three auditors of the Envoy of Barátá heard, and it might be said that they listened to the sound of a bomb that burst before the hour they had had in mind; but the metaphor would not be exact, for the bursting of a bomb is a sudden sound, and now comprehension came only gradually to astonished minds. As it did, they saw that they were confronted by something different from the anticipations which they had discussed and with which they had planned to deal.

Dr. Dalston might have been foolish, officious, even treacherous, in what he had said to President Gómez. He might have offered some bargain beyond his authority, or some surrender to the threat of that approaching ship which President Cortéz certainly would not approve. But, however these things might be, it must be their part today to concur, to approve, even to praise.

In the end, it would make no difference at all, for the negotiations were not destined to last to a further day; but the immediate necessity was that there should be amity among themselves, and that Dr. Dalston should have no excuse for declining to visit the Garden of Many Plants in the cool of the evening hour.

"You mean," Señor Philipo asked, "that it is a ship over which you have wireless control?"

"That was what I meant."

"And the captain would obey a radio message from you, changing his course?"

"It might not be done quite as crudely as that, but it is substantially true."

"And you threatened President Gómez with this?" Señor Philipo, feeling his way cautiously on unknown and unexpected ground, was yet genuinely puzzled as to what had occurred, and why.

"I did not threaten. I mentioned what the position is."

"Yet even to mention that must have the sound of a threat."

"I thought not. I suggested that it might be done by common consent."

"To which, I fear, President Gómez would not agree?"

A smile curved Señor Philipo's mobile lips as he asked this, having no doubt at all what the answer would be. Let them offer what terms they would, President Gómez would prefer the guarantees which machine-guns give. Yet suppose that he had appeared to yield—or even seen that he had no option but to do so—before the power which Dr. Dalston had convinced him that he certainly held?

That was a possibility not to be ignored. And, if that were so, might not the President be already arranging for the assassination which they were going to such needless trouble to carry out in his name! With a bewildering reversal of that which had been in their minds before, Señor Philipo saw their envoy as one to be guarded at any cost—at least until this most unsuspected power should have been used the right way!

"Excellency," he said, and he used the formal title now without the note of sarcasm which his voice had held on the previous night, "now that you have let the Government of Bioli know that you can do them so great an injury, you will do well to remain within the Legation walls, or to move abroad with a great care, for you have a life which it would be easy to lose."

Dr. Dalston laughed. "Do you take it so? I would judge it a better way. Do you not forget that we are offering most, if not all, of that which they could hope to win by a ruinous and most doubtful war?"

Señor Philipo paused again. To those who knew the hollowness of the offers which were being made, it was hard to give them even that doubtful value which they might have in President Gómez's hesitant mind, but he saw that Dr. Dalston might regard them with more respect. Yet, without disturbing the serenity of their envoy's mind, he felt that the warning must be impressed.

"I fear," he said, "that you must not judge President Gómez (for whose abilities I have the highest respect) with—may I say it without offence?—the simplicity of an English mind. He is very subtle in all he does, and may impute to others a subtlety even an insincerity—like his own."

Enrico was not sure that this judgment was widely wrong, nor, in justice to President Gómez, would he overlook that there might be reason for caution or disbelief when listening to the professions of Baratá. He had to recognise, beyond that, that there had been an atmosphere of some reserve on the President's part at the interview of which they spoke. But he knew that, even while he listened, Juliana might be disclosing the bond which now attached him so closely to Bioli, and most particularly to the personal interests of the President's family. He did not intend to mention this, which was to be made public in such time and manner as Juliana and her father might prefer, but it gave assurance to his reply: "It may be all as you judge, but, on this occasion, I feel some confidence that what I said will be taken in the right way."

Señor Serati, whose thoughts had been no less busy because his lips had been closed, had come to a point approaching incredulity regarding the whole tale. Accustomed to an atmosphere of habitual falsehood, amidst which those who wished for a long life must disentangle sufficient truth for its protection, he felt here, with a sound instinct, that there must be something—probably something vital—they did not know. He asked, with an outward smoothness which was more difficult to him than to Señor Philipo to maintain: "Señor, would you make it more clear than it is to me why you should have told this to President Gómez at all?"

Enrico, feeling that he had the situation well under control, and conscious of more than one trump still unplayed from a strong hand, was disposed to toy for a time with men whom he did not trust, and whose mystification he thought that he understood (though it would have been a shock indeed to know what their actual problem was), and answered with an argument which might have had force to those whose bargains were sealed by honour rather than baser considerations: "It appeared to me that, as President Gómez would have no use for munitions for which he had paid a very large sum, he would welcome an arrangement by which they could be realised in another market."

Señor Philipo's glance across the table at his colleagues was plain in its urgency that the interrogation should be left to him, though Señor Serati's query bad been opportune enough, and the reply had been interesting to hear. He asked: "You could arrange that?"

"Probably. Though there might be some loss. I have little doubt that a customer could be found for the cargo who would pay approximately, if not fully, the original price."

Señor Philipo saw that this was likely enough. There were more than one or two Central and South American states which would be glad to bargain for cargo of munitions that found its way on to the high seas, and could now be bought without difficult questions of export licences, or the reasons for such a purchase, having to be overcome.

If—it was a small, but not an absolutely incredible possibility—President Gómez had been brought to a firm belief in the good faith of the treaty which was now being negotiated, he might not be unwilling to consider selling the cargo, in such a way (which would be almost a routine method of Latin-American finance) that, whereas the purchase price had come out of Bioli's treasury, the proceeds would go into his personal account.

Señor Philipo's suavity had become almost genial as he asked: "The President, do we understand, entertained the proposal favourably?"

"He will, I feel sure, give it his favourable consideration."

Enrico, still with the unplayed, unsuspected trumps in a hand which he regarded as overwhelming in strength, watched with some curiosity to see how this assurance would be received. If, he thought, they had been sincere in their negotiations, it would mean little to them, but otherwise very much. In fact, their reactions puzzled him. Behind their practised reserve, he felt that they were puzzled, even embarrassed, rather than either indifferent, or pleased by the news they heard.

So, in fact, both Señors Philipo and Serati were. Their final conclusion, on hearing that Dr. Dalston could divert the cargo, had been that he must be kept alive, and that his assassination would have been a disastrous blunder, into which they had almost stumbled.

But now they saw a further and even more fascinating possibility. If Enrico should be persuaded or coerced into diverting the cargo without Bioli's consent, it might be well enough, and he might be assassinated on a later day. But the incident might have become public to a degree which would give it an ugly look, even to providing Bioli with a measure of justification for the crime which was to be attributed to it. But if President Gómez could be persuaded to give his consent to the diversion of the cargo, and then, when it had been done with his own proper authority, and Bioli had become most helpless to face her foes, the Envoy of Baratá should be wickedly blown apart—well, the whole event would have a neatness of which plotters may dream, but which they do not often achieve in their waking hours!

And then, in a casual conversational tone, as though he said no more than that it was a fine day, Enrico dropped on them a second bomb, and one more devastating than that could be which Conradi had constructed with such loving care that it would go far toward breaking his heart if it should not be used at last for its purposed end. (But, listening silently to this conversation, and remembering how definite the instructions of President Cortéz had been, Conradi still had a good hope that those orders might not be changed.)

"Señor," Enrico said, "if I proposed that the cargo of the *Billy Winch* should not be wasted by being brought to a country of settled peace, it may not have been as impertinent as you were disposed, at the first hearing, to judge, for, as I think you already know, I am of a mind to make a home in Baratá, that being my mother's land; and where a man makes his home I think his investments should be; so that I am disposed to consult with our own President when we return to San Cristóval as to how a sum which we might put tentatively at two hundred thousand pounds could be invested there. And, because Bioli is the country of my own birth, I may be inclined to support it with a substantial, though smaller amount. If I plan this, and…"—he suggested vaguely—"…perhaps to bind myself to these countries by other ties, may I not be concerned that this should be done on a basis of settled peace, from which the helm of the *Billy Winch* should be turned aside?"

Enrico regarded his auditors, and he had no occasion to fear that his words had been offered to careless ears. He had produced a confusion of feelings over which the mask of diplomacy had become difficult to adjust. How are eyes and lips to be controlled when you cannot instantly be sure of the expression they ought to wear, to conceal the chaos of anticipation and consternation within?

Two hundred thousand pounds, which, in a few hours would have been blown away on the smoke of a bomb a thousand pesetas would dearly buy!

Two hundred thousand pounds to be invested in Baratá, which was President Cortéz, which was also themselves! Indirectly, how much of that stream of wealth might not percolate down to their own pockets? Even directly, a commission of five thousand pounds (if not ten!) would be reasonable to require, and a favour which the President would find it hard to refuse.

So thought Señors Philipo and Serati, being on this occasion, "two minds with but a single thought, two hearts that beat as one."

Only Señor Conradi sat apparently unmoved. He had a direct and literal mind. He remembered the explicit instructions he had received. He still thought that his loving labour would not be lost.

Señor Philipo was first to speak. He had rapidly adjusted his attitude. The incident which was to have ended Dr. Dalston's life was not to be merely delayed. It must be put indefinitely aside. But that, when President Cortéz knew the position, would arrange itself. And he could be reached on the telephone in three minutes at any time. It is true that conversations carried on by that medium would be tapped by Bioli, but, now that President Gómez had been informed of Dr. Dalston's intentions, that scarcely mattered. Communications could be almost frank! Except, of course, on one point. But that could be understood in discreet and sufficient words.

So Señor Philipo swiftly resolved. And, more immediately, he saw that it would be a mistake to receive the news of the proposed investment with professions either of too lively gratitude or surprise. A man should be congratulated when he decides to invest his wealth in a prudent and productive channel.

"Excellency," he said, "it is a wise decision, which is pleasure to hear. The undeveloped resources of Baratá (and even of Bioli) are very great. It is only capital which they require. You will, I suppose, build a fortune for yourself, and a memory which will long endure. When you hint at other ties, may I venture without impertinence to conclude that the Señorita Juliana is meant?"

"You will observe," Enrico smiled, "that I mentioned none. Yet there might be a less probable guess."

He rose as he spoke. He thought that his colleagues would like an opportunity for discussion among themselves, which he was willing for them to have. He made an easy guess that the long-distance telephone would soon be in use. He saw no objection to that, though he did not surmise that it would be upon an issue of life and death, in which he himself would be primarily involved.

CHAPTER TWENTY-ONE

THE RETICENCE OF ANOTHER PRESIDENT

THERE was a moment's silence after Dr. Dalston withdrew, which Señor Serati broke. There were occasions when he would be silent before strangers, letting Señor Philipo speak, for he realised that the ex-envoy had the suaver manner; but among themselves he had a more dominant tongue.

"It is plain," he said, "we must let him live. Conradi, you must save yourself for a better time."

Conradi gave him a blank stare. "I do not know," he said, "what you mean. I am an Officer of Customs, whose knowledge has been at your service, and that of His Excellency the Envoy of Baratá. "

"You know well what I mean," Señor Serati replied, with some impatience in his voice, for there had been a lack of courtesy, if nothing worse, in the tone in which Señor Conradi had addressed him. "Caution is to be praised, but it can be used to excess when we are alone and not liable to be overheard. And we are aware what your orders are."

"I cannot tell of what you may be aware, but my orders are not given by, nor to be discussed with, you."

Señor Philipo, stroking a smooth but swarthy chin, saw that an open quarrel was near to come between two men whose mutual dislike, before this, had been easy to see. Now he interposed while Señor Serati paused upon an angry reply. "But, Señor Conradi, if we report these matters of importance, of which we have just heard, to our President, you will not say we are wrong; and, after that, you will be willing to speak to him?"

"I will speak to him if he summon me to do so. I will not call him up, for my instructions are not of that kind. There are too many words here for which I can see no occasion at all."

As Conradi said this, he made it plain that there would be no more words exchanged with him at that time, either bad or good, for he rose abruptly, reaching the door as he ended his curt reply.

Señor Serati followed him with an angry stare. He said: "The rogue presumes. It is the way to a quick end."

"So he may, and so it may be," Señor Philipo replied, in his most placable tone, "but in this case I would not say he is wholly wrong. I have no doubt that he had orders from our President that he should keep a still tongue, even with us, and, perhaps, that he should not communicate directly with him, be his dilemma the worst it might. If that be so, it is no more than his obedience requires that the President should summon him to speak, rather than that he should ask for fresh orders in a way which might be misinterpreted by those who would overhear.

"But what difference for us is there in that? We will inform the President of what we have learnt, and you can trust that he will make sure that Conradi will be instructed aright, in such a manner as his present orders require."

Señor Serati did not dispute this. He had come to have another aspect of the problem upon his mind.

"It is plain," he said, "that Dalston must live until he has given orders that the cargo shall be turned aside, and even longer, until he will have made these investments of which he talks, so that the money is in our own banks, from which it will not be easy for it to be taken away. But, until then—which may be for many weeks, if not months—is this treaty which we are now making to stand? Or will Dalston, having as much concern—if not more—for this country as Baratá, be content for us to make a mock of that which he has been instrumental to do?"

Señor Philipo did not dispute that there was a problem here, but he thought it to be no more than that with which their President would be equal to deal.

They both saw that from the moment when the *Billy Winch* should be ordered to change its destination from San Luíz to another port, Bioli would be again at the mercy of Baratá, as it had been in previous times. But as to how Dr. Dalston might be kept content till his use was done, without the treaty being put into actual operation, Señor Philipo was sanguine, though somewhat vague. He thought that President Gómez would be equal to overcoming the difficulty.

At the back of his fertile though otherwise reprehensible mind he had already formulated an idea which might, at the right moment, be suggested to President Cortéz. But why mention it now? It would make it more than probable that it would be first proposed from Señor Serati's lips, and Señor Philipo preferred to have the full credit for his useful ideas.

This one was that President Gómez might declare, at the last moment, that the matter was of too great importance to be settled by him, or his Government, without endorsement of the popular vote. A plebiscite must be held!

There would be no danger in that. It is not only in Central Europe that it is possible to foretell in advance what the result of a plebiscite will be. That is necessary, for otherwise how could any government feel secure? And there would be the further advantage that (if it should be decided that the plebiscite should show a majority adverse to the scheme), it would be a fair-sounding reason for its rejection, and if Bioli (without its cargo of arms) were to make the rebuff occasion for war—well, there would be little to fear from that!

Certainly, it was far too good an idea to be spilled randomly about, where Señor Serati could pick it up. But it gave Señor Philipo confidence that they progressed on a road which was firm to tread, and he was sufficiently detached from that which had become a settled plan in his colleague's less ductile mind, to observe that, unless Dr. Dalston should be too awkward regarding such developments to be comfortably endured, it might not be necessary to remove him at all.

Leaving that to the future, he approached the delicate question of which of them should undertake the enviable part of acquainting

President Cortéz with the good news that the *Billy Winch* could be turned aside, and of the golden rain which was to descend upon the parched finances of Baratá.

It was a telephone conversation to be carried on without privacy, on more than one matter of delicacy, which he knew himself to be the fitter to undertake, and he thought also that he had the better right. But the latter point was one to which he did not expect that Señor Serati would agree, nor did he suppose that he would readily resign his claim, it being so obviously advantageous to be the first communicant of such happy news.

But in this he found that he had feared a difficulty which would not arise. Señor Serati was politely willing to concede the honour to him, suggesting only that, as the President must be informed, sooner or later, of the fatality of the night, it might be expedient to use that event as the occasion of the call, letting other matters follow, as being mentioned at an opportunity to which they were incidental only.

Señor Philipo agreed readily to this, understanding, without the clumsiness of words, that a bargain has been proposed.

The death of Pedro, whatever its cause might be, was of no interest to Bioli, nor any business of its police. He had been a citizen of Baratá, and had come to his end within the Legation walls, which were Baratá territory according to the usage of international law. It was therefore primarily a matter with which the envoy in residence should deal. But Dr. Dalston had shown no more than a perfunctory interest in the matter. In his ignorance of the office he had held for so short a time, he might not even be aware of the responsibility which was his.

Beyond him, there was the ultimate authority of the President of Baratá, and it was desirable that he should be informed in the right way.

Señor Serati might be an entirely innocent man (as we know he was), but he was no less aware that the event might be laid at his own door. Indeed, in the mouths of gossip, if not in more responsible deliberations, it was a simple guess that he would be considered the murderer of a man who had gained a position so confidential that it might well have become embarrassing, or abused. Those who become the depositories of the dubious secrets of more powerful men may often find, in their last hours, that the profits of such intimacy are inadequate for the perils which they entail.

Against this probability, there should at least be a plausible, officially-accepted account of how Pedro had come to lie in the hall with a broken neck, which should be all that the case required. President Cortéz would be unlikely to concern himself much about Pedro's end, be it from whatever cause, unless, of course, he should be seeking excuse to make trouble for Señor Serati, which the Minister of Health saw no present occasion to apprehend.

But there was a separate reason for caution in the fact that the President might consider Señor Serati to have applied disciplinary action to one of his own retinue at an inopportune time and place. Knowing the vital importance of the construction which was to be put upon Dr. Dalston's assassination, the President of Baratá might hold it to be an unpardonable intrusion upon his personal affairs for Señor Serati to complicate the position with a previous homicide within the Legation walls.

But if the incident were put as an accidental occurrence in a convincing manner, such questions would not arise; and on that point Señor Serati judged soundly that the President would more readily accept assurances from Señor Philipo's lips than his, and, after that, there would be news of such importance as might well put aside the incident of Pedro's death for the triviality that it surely was.

So, on this understanding, clearly bargained in sparing words, Señor Philipo instructed the First Secretary to establish telephone connection with President Cortéz at his Residency in San Cristóval. There was some delay about this, for the President showing no alacrity in responding to the invitation. He was, his secretary announced, busily engaged. But a message could be taken to him.

It was an initial difficulty at which Señor Philipo was not surprised. He knew that the President, who could be fluent enough on what he considered to be suitable occasions, recognised the more frequent virtues of silence, and would be far more likely to approve the reticence of Conradi than Señor Serati's blunter speech. And on a telephone line which was liable—which was almost certain!—to be tapped. No, President Cortéz has other occupations, which he preferred.

But Señor Philipo knew that he had a matter of urgency to convey. It had been urgent before, but Conradi's intransigence had made it tenfold more so. Would President Cortéz forgive anyone concerned if they should allow the assassination of Dr. Dalston without informing him of his unanticipated generosity and his unsuspected power?

Anticipating the difficulty, Señor Philipo was prepared to overcome it. The uses of Pedro should not cease with his death. He said vaguely: "Tell the President that there has been a fatality within the Legation, of which I think he should be informed."

"A fatality! Shall I not inform His Excellency who is dead?"

Señor Philipo was curt: "I am the one to judge of what is for his own ears. You will tell him what I have said."

It was no more than a few minutes later that Señor Philipo heard President Cortéz enquire with ungracious brevity: "What is it you wish to say?"

The short delay had allowed time for President Gómez to be connected also. An unknown, if not unsuspected auditor, he had the benefit of the conversation which followed.

"I thought that you should know that Serati's man, Pedro, died during the night."

"*Died?* That is Serati's concern, rather than mine. What happened?"

"He fell downstairs during the night and fractured his skull."

There was a moment's silence. The statement had a crudely improbable sound. But the President reflected that the conversation might be intended for other ears rather than his. He must respond now in such a manner as to render it easy for Señor Philipo to establish whatever version of the incident it might seem wise to publish abroad. There might be another tale to be told at another time, in another way.

"How," he asked, "did he come to do that?"

"No one can certainly say. It was at an hour when everyone else in the Legation was asleep. It is supposed that he heard, or thought he heard, a noise in the night, and went to assure himself with no more light than the moon gave; and that he must have fallen down stairs which he did not see."

"What view of the matter does Doctor Dalston take?"

"He does not appear greatly interested, but he agrees that that is the most probable explanation."

"Then," the President thought, "he must be an even simpler man than I judged him before," but it was not the occasion for such reflections to be spoken aloud. He said: "Well, Serati must get another to guard his back when he walks abroad. But you must think the man of an importance to me that he never had, that you should call me for such a tale."

"You will excuse me that I was wrong. Apart from that, I cannot say that I have justification for disturbing you. Everything here goes well, and Doctor Dalston is naturally pleased that he has been the means of negotiating what he described yesterday as a treaty of peace between the two countries.

"He mentioned at breakfast this morning that he has finally decided to make his home here, or in Baratá. I don't think it is only that he likes the country. He sees its economic possibilities. He was talking of investing as much as two hundred thousand pounds in Baratá, if we would advise him how it could be most profitably employed."

"How much did you say?"

"Two hundred thousand pounds."

"It is an amount with which he could do much in a land of such undeveloped resources as ours. You can congratulate him on better judgment than many have."

"He has been largely influenced, as he said, by the fact that the old quarrel between the two countries is being ended. He has made a point, I believe, of some arms which Bioli is importing being transferred to another destination, and I believe he is finding President Gómez a customer for them so that no loss will occur."

"A customer? How can he do that?"

"That is more than I am exactly informed. He might say that it is not precisely business of ours. But I suppose it may have some connection with the fact that he controls most of the shipping that sails between England and the Central American ports."

"*Most* of the shipping? You must put it too high when you say that."

"Perhaps I do. It is evident that he is not controlling them while he is here. But he mentioned in conversation this morning that he had controlling interests in the S.A.A. and the Forward lines."

There was a moment's pause, which Señor Philipo was patient not to interrupt by speaking again. He expected that what he had said would take some digestion, and he knew that he had left much to his hearer's imagination; but he was anxious not to disclose more than he must (or than President Gómez already knew) on the ambiguous privacy of that long-distance wire. He thought he had said enough to demonstrate the inexpediency of assassinating a man who might be most useful alive, and that President Cortéz would have no difficulty in communicating that conclusion in words which would be free from sinister significance to those who might overhear.

President Cortéz was not too dull to know what the pause meant, or what he would be expected to say; but when his words came they were of an unexpected significance: "It is information which it has been pleasant to hear. It is also pleasant to observe that the plans which we had already formed for the future relations of Bioli and Baratá will not be discordant to Doctor Dalston's personal aims."

What might be the meaning of that? It might be taken as a hint that the President would not allow anything he had heard to induce him to change his plans, but to find an opposite meaning was to impose upon ambiguity a strain which it would not bear. And Señor Philipo had heard a note of finality in the words, threatening that he might be cut off next moment with no better guidance than that! Certainly, to repeat the cryptic pronouncement to Andreas Conradi would be unlikely to persuade him to hold his hand. Did the President expect a more leading question from him? Giving evidence of his lively mind, Señor Philipo answered with no perceptible pause:

"It is fortunate, as you say. It is fitting that he should share our prosperity who has helped to establish peace. But you will allow that others have done their part. We have been indebted in particular to the able assistance of Señor Conradi, whose detailed knowledge of the matters with which we dealt was a vital aid. Perhaps a word of appreciation from yourself on this occasion would not be too much to suggest, and would, I am sure, be highly valued by a quiet and sensitive man."

Faintly over the wire there came a hardly suppressed expletive; "Imbecile!" which Señor Philipo, flushing with a natural indignation, recognised that he was not expected to hear. Then, after a moment's silence, the President's voice asked sharply: "Why should I do that? Can he not have proper thanks at a more suitable time?" And then, with an impatient reluctance, real or assumed: "But if you have led him to expect—I would not have him hurt, if he has done well. Let him come, if you can call him without keeping me here."

"He will be here with no moment's delay," Señor Philipo answered, hoping that it would be true, for he had no exact knowledge of where Conradi might be, but for once the fates were kind to a harassed man. It was no more than sixty seconds later that Andreas Conradi took up the receiver. He had been at hand, and had shown neither enthusiasm nor reluctance to take the call.

Now he heard: "I am told by Señor Philipo that you have given him and his colleagues expert and diligent assistance, so that they recommend you for praise."

"Excellency, I have done no more than my duty was."

"There are many who do less. If you continue with such diligence to carry out the duties you have undertaken, you will not be unrewarded at last."

"Excellency, I thank—" But there was no object in further words. President Cortéz had cut him off.

CHAPTER TWENTY-TWO

CONRADI WILL USE HIS BOMB

THE sky was a cloudless blue; the sun continued to rise. Obviously, it must be hot; and there was no humidity in the air, even after the deluge of the last day. The sandy ground sucked it in, and parted dry lips, asking for more.

Yet the effect of the rain had not passed. It had given a sudden, transient vivid tone to the forest greens, that would be sombrely dark again by the next day, as their habit was in the dry months. It gave an exhilaration to man and beast, which was felt by their free-striding horses, as well as by Enrico and Juliana, who had other causes for lightness of heart and limb, riding together upon the hills, as they had agreed to do, so soon as they could make their escapes from the morning meal.

Was it by some deep compensating law that the one whose death had been callously planned for an hour which was now so near rode full of the joy of life, and the intoxication of love, while those by whom he was doomed were anxious, quarrelling men, surely having no pleasure in what they did, if we make exception of Conradi— Conradi who listened unmoved to Señor Serati's angry sarcasm and Señor Philipo's suaver arguments, saying only: " It is your part to get him to the Garden of Many Plants. You have no concern beyond that. I take my orders from the President, not from you."

Conradi was not even sullen in meeting the repeated, even abusive protests of the two men. He had one thing to say, which he thought enough. He took his orders from the President, not from them. He professed to have no doubt of what those orders were, and

Señor Philipo, going over every carefully memorised word of the conversation he had had himself, found it hard to doubt that the man said no more than the truth was, however inexplicable it might be.

Yet there was so much at stake, both in the fate of the *Billy Winch* and the wealth which certainly would not be used to the advantage of Baratá by Dr. Dalston's heirs, if he himself should be destroyed in the Garden of Many Plants, that Señors Serati and Philipo were of one mind that, whatever the President's orders might be, the assassination must be deferred. In two days' time a letter could reach San Cristóval, and a written answer be returned. That was the safer way. It might avoid an irreparable error. Señor Serati said, with undeniable truth, that a man can always be killed. If you let him live by mistake, it is an error which can be put right on the next day. But if you kill him, and then regret—well, so you may, but there is nothing more to be done.

Conradi did not dispute this, but it was not his concern. He had his orders to carry out.

So he might have, Señor Philipo suavely agreed, but had they been for a particular day? Conradi must admit that they had not! They had been for the earliest suitable occasion? Agreed. But there had been a point of urgency then, because the occasion of quarrel was to precede the landing of the cargo of arms, which might now be diverted through the delay.

Conradi was equally willing to admit the force of this argument. But it did not move him at all. He had been told nothing of the *Billy Winch* or other matters which had been subjects of conversation since he arrived. He had been ordered to use a bomb in such a way that it would appear to be the work of the enemies of Baratá, and the consequences were not his concern.

So the talk went on, he saying little, and they much; and the two who rode in the hills may have talked less, being often on narrow paths, where it would have been foolish to ride abreast, and on steep descents where there must be alertness of eye, and of hand on a taut rein, but when they did, it was talk of a better kind.

For them, the sun of life rose to shine on a path of flowers, stretching fairly ahead now that the first barriers had been broken through.

Last night, as he made his way along the silent, moonlit streets, Enrico had thought that, if the merciful Fates would but guard his steps until he came to that shadowed door which Juliana would leave ajar, he would ask no more of life which would have been so ecstatically fulfilled. Did he think that now? Not at all. Life had become a rich feast of which no more than the first morsel had reached his lips. It had a value he had not adequately supposed, and its loss a peril correspondingly great. But it was a loss of which he had little fear. He had gained a conquering confidence in himself and the destiny that was his, in this first exultation of love consummated and returned. It was a mood which armed him well against many of the dangers of life, but what use could it be against Conradi's bomb? There could be no more than the bare chance of a faulty detonator or fuse, over which he had no control—and Conradi's bombs were not known to fail.

Juliana's mood was akin to his. She had no premonition of grief. The doubts she had once had of Enrico's safety had faded, now that she understood the power that was in his hands and the application that it would have. He might be buying at a high price, but it was not reasonable to doubt that his own security would be among the assets for which he paid.

And her father had been kind. He had approved her choice. He had even condoned the impetuosity of the secret marriage. Only, he had stipulated that the secret should not be disclosed. A formal engagement must be announced, and a public wedding fitting to her position could follow in as short a time as could be fairly arranged.

And meanwhile? Juliana had coaxed. In the end, the President, seeing advantages to Bioli, and perhaps to himself in the course of coming events as he (reasonably, but quite incorrectly) foresaw them, and being in a consequent good humour, had yielded to one whom he could seldom deny. He had agreed to contemn diplomatic and social conventions by inviting the Envoy of Baratá to reside for a time at the Palazzo, on the pretext that the Legation building must be inconveniently crowded while his colleagues were there, and perhaps also using the argument that the President desired special opportunities for conferring with him upon the new era of friendship between the two countries which he had been so largely instrumental in bringing about.

Enrico heard with a natural pleasure. He saw Juliana, not for the first time, to be one who would not be easily baulked. She had a tenacity of will which he was not likely to blame when it won for them that which was their equal desire. But, beyond that, he saw that she might be a potent ally for the coming days which his hope forecast. Strength of will would be ruled by love, and a loyalty which he could not doubt.

It was a vain dream. The invitation to the Palazzo would never lead to the happy days in its walls which they lightly dreamed, and the happier nights, when they thought to secretly meet in the silent hours, would never come. But, by the mercy of Heaven, men do not foresee the storm when the skies are clear, or guess correctly when the lightning will strike. They had the joy of the hour.

"Is there any trouble about the man you knocked down the stairs?" Juliana asked, as they came to a path, level and high, where they could ride abreast with no care.

"No. He was found dead in the hall with a broken skull. They are puzzled, but what can they do more than guess—and that wrong? I looked at him myself, and gave an easy opinion that he had fallen down the stairs in the night, and died from a fractured skull. They could see that for themselves. But when I talked of the *Billy Winch*, and of investments I was anxious to make, they had no mind left for such trifles as a dead man. I am sorry I killed him, but he was meddling in matters with which he had no proper concern, and the knife which was still in his hand when he was found showed what he might have done to me if I had argued in a less forcible manner."

"Unless you had gone back to your room, which was all he asked you to do!"

"*All?* Do you think I should have done that, merely because the man had a knife?"

"I don't know. You have just said you are sorry for what you did." Juliana's voice had a petulant tone. Her eyes mocked.

"I said I was sorry I killed him. I didn't mean to do that."

"Well, it was a rude thing to say. You should have been glad! He would have talked, if he had lived, and made more trouble than he was worth—and perhaps trouble for me, if he had followed you, as he would have been likely to do."

"Then I will say I am glad. And he was a slimy brute. He may have had his uses for Serati, but even he took his death very cheerfully."

"So do I," she said, "and so any sensible person would." There was no doubt of her own cheerfulness, which it would have taken much more than a dead Pedro to overcast. Enrico wondered whether she spoke deliberately thus, thinking that he might have some scruples of conscience for the manslaughter he had committed, which she was anxious to argue away; but he judged more accurately that it was a matter which really seemed small to her. One for their mutual satisfaction, and his own praise. She might be disposed to value human life rather by the standards of this country to which she was native than those of the England where her youth had been spent. Or perhaps it would be fairer to say that she regarded human lives as of a very variable account. And is there no reason in that?

She turned the conversation next moment upon the projected visit to the Garden of Many Plants, which he had said that he would avoid if he could. In his present mood, he counted all hours wasted which were not with her; and though he had some knowledge of healing plants, and had expressed curiosity concerning the flora of the New World in his first conversation with Señor Serati, he would have preferred to explore the treasures the Gardens held at another time, and in other company. His colleagues must be tolerated courteously during the hours of diplomatic negotiations. It was another matter to make them the companions of leisure hours.

"Still," Juliana said sensibly, "you must go. It is the penalty of the high office you hold that you cannot do as you will in such matters as that. You have no good cause to refuse, and to do so now, with less than that, would not only be rude to them, but to Bioli, which makes the Garden of Many Plants its most confident boast. It is the one thing it has which even Rio, or Buenos Aires, could not excel."

"You can contrive to be there?"

"I am afraid not. My father would be sure to object, and he has conceded so much that it would be a poor return to ask for a foolish thing, or to do that of which he would hear later and disapprove.

"You see, the Gardens will be so reserved that they will be practically closed. The police were ordered to guard you with special care from the first day when you arrived (that is, during the day; they do not expect you to slip out of the Legation during the night I), and such precautions will not be less now that you are talking of bringing your English money for investment here, as well as in Baratá. If I should go there this afternoon, it would be a most conspicuous thing, which would be remarked. It would be said that I followed you in immodest ways. If our engagement were announced almost immediately afterwards, the talk would be more, not less. For it is not the custom here for girls to pursue men, as they do in Europe with little shame. We do not woo here, we are wooed."

As she said this her eyes laughed into his, making them both aware that she had shown the girls of Bioli to be no less capable than those of Europe to pluck the fruit they desire, though they may have some differences of technique which appear important to them. But he saw that there was reason in what she said, and gave way none the less readily when she added: "And what difference will it make? You will find a note from my father at the Legation when you get back, inviting you to the Palazzo tonight. But you can delay to come till tomorrow, if you have more to collect than can be brought in a shorter time."

"Yes," he replied, in a manner that mocked her own, "you can be well assured that I shall do that."

They jested in the happy spirit of youth, conscious of the close accord that can venture thus without peril of hurt or offence. And meanwhile, in the Legation's wide-windowed lounge, the bickering of the last two hours had ended in victory for a stubborn man.

It had not been easily gained, for Señors Philipo and Serati were men of diplomatic resource, and there appeared to them to be so much at stake that they were resolved not to give way. They had told Conradi plainly that they would thwart him, if they must, by guarding the Envoy themselves from his attempts, until a written answer from President Cortéz could be received.

Conradi had muttered and frowned, and asked at last: "How will you do that?"

"We can persuade him," Señor Philipo replied, "to remain here, where there would be no object in procuring his death, for it would be plain that it had been done by us, there not being even a servant here who is not a native of Baratá. Or, if he go abroad, we can keep at his side. I suppose you would not dare to destroy us also, and expect the President's praise?"

"I do nothing," Conradi replied, "beyond what my orders are. But if you are warned, and still will not draw apart, should you say that he would blame me?"

It was a question about which they could not avoid some doubt, and one which they had no appetite to have solved in the only possible way

"Well," Señor Philipo replied, "if you would go so far, we must make the more effort to keep him here. We shall, at least, cancel the arrangement for this afternoon, so you may put away any plan you have made for using your bomb in the Garden of Many Plants."

Conradi did look disconcerted by that, even beyond what he could be expected to feel. He seemed for a moment to be without a reply, but then he said: "You can stay here, if you will. I do not see how I could alter that, but I do not see how you could prevent Doctor Dalston going, or me either. What will you gain by staying here?"

At this point, Señor Serati rose. "I am resolved what I will do. I will telephone to President Cortéz again."

Señor Philipo looked doubtful. "I am not sure that you will get much by that. It would need a plain talk, which you cannot have. Conradi should recognise how we stand."

He remembered his own rebuff; but after saying this, he made no further objection, being anxious that every chance should be tried; and if Señor Serati were blamed for an indiscretion, it would not touch him, after the protest which he had made.

Señor Serati got through to the President easily enough. He had more difficulty in beginning his conversation in a natural manner. He said: "Excellency, we have some discussion with Conradi, of which we think you should know. Now that the draft treaty has been sent for your approval, we have told him that nothing more is to be done until it be returned with your observations thereon. But there are new points of which he is thinking from time to time, which he would have us open to the Bioli Committee, which we suppose it would be confusing, at this moment, to do.

"But we will write you thereon, and meanwhile will you tell him, with your own lips, that there is nothing more to do of *any kind* till we have had your reply?"

President Cortéz appeared to be stirred by this question to an anger which he was at less care to conceal than he had been on the earlier occasion. He called Serati a pig of particularly repulsive habits, without lowering his voice. He asked: "Are you all mad today? I have nothing more to say to Conradi, either bad or good. When he left, he had instructions from me, which were quite simple, and which I see no occasion to change, or to explain. If he cannot obey without worrying you or me, I must have chosen the wrong man. Tell him that, and that I have no occasion to speak to him at all. "

"Regarding Doctor Dalston...," Señor Serati began, ignoring, in the extremity of the emergency, the insult he had received, but he was interrupted with: "Serati, I am busy. I do not understand why I am called up on such needless pretext. Be good enough to write." The connection was cut off abruptly.

The Minister of Health of the Republic of Baratá put down the receiver, an angry and baffled man. He knew President Cortéz, if his temper failed, to be of unmeasured speech, but he had never been addressed in such a manner since he had been elevated to the exalted office he now held. He was shrewd enough to recognise, and sanguine enough to hope, that the President's anger had been put on for the misleading of anyone who might be listening in, but there was only a limited satisfaction in that, for no man likes to be addressed with the epithets he had received in the hearing of others he knows not whom. Nor could he see that there had been any wisdom in the President's outburst, from whatever angle it might be considered, nor conspicuous prudence in his closing words. (This was a doubt that came to President Cortéz almost at the same moment, but on reflection, and knowing more than Señor Serati guessed, he decided that he had said nothing he would recall.)

But these minor questions were obliterated from Señor Serati's mind as he recognised that the query he had not dared to put into plain words had been answered beyond misunderstanding, and in such a way that there could be no remaining excuse for obstructing, even for a sufficient interval to allow of letters being exchanged, that which Conradi had been charged to do. No offer of loans from Dr. Dalston, no hope that the helm of the *Billy Winch* might be turned toward another shore, would induce President Cortéz to change the instructions on which Conradi was so urgent to act. To oppose them longer might be to risk disgrace, even assassination, on returning to Baratá. What virtue was there in any investments by Dr. Dalston, however large, or in any settlement with Bioli, either by methods of peace or war, if he himself should be shut out from participation in their rewards? None at all.

Señor Philipo looked at it in the same way. Anticipating that Serati would gain little from his telephone effort, the ex-envoy had spent the time with his usual diplomatic caution, and with a diplomatic ability which may be the envy of simpler men, in driving a bargain with Conradi, by which, if Serati's effort should fail, as they agreed to expect it would, Serati and he would give their co-operation to the incident which was to occur in the Garden of Many Plants, in consideration of a harmless document which Conradi was to sign.

"*I take my orders,*" Señor Philipo wrote, in a small, neat hand, the letters thinly drawn as a spider's thread, "*from President Cortéz, and none but him,*" and passed it across the table, where, with a frowning reluctance, the signature *Andreas Conradi* was added, in an equally neat, though somewhat bolder script.

Conradi watched the paper, as though grudging that it should exist, while Señor Philipo folded it squarely and inserted it in his breast-pocket. The eyes of the man who loved silence, and seldom wrote anything more compromising than the customs records of his official duties rested upon the pocket as though memorising where the document had been placed, and considering how it could be recovered. He was another who wondered whether he had been indiscreet, and decided in his own favour, though not without hesitation. But Señor Philipo considered that he had insured himself against responsibility for any error which might occur, and, beyond that, he felt some confidence that the President must have good reason for what he did. President Cortéz had never been a man of his hands, being too grossly fat. But in several crises of his adventurous life he had shown capacity to guard his head, and outwit his foes, in unexpected ways, such as Señor Philipo could admire. It seemed unlikely that he would be acting without solid reason now.

CHAPTER TWENTY-THREE

DEATH COMES IN THE
GARDEN OF MANY PLANTS

THEY were nearly two hours in the Garden of Many Plants. They had one of its directors for guide. An elderly, amicable, learned, short-sighted man, whose sensitive fingers would caress at times the leaves of the plants of which he spoke, as though the sense of touch had become a surer guide than his failing sight. Señor Philipo, watchful to stage-manage the tragedy which was to come, as he had now agreed with Conradi to do, saw no danger in this doddering botanist, as he called him in a contemptuous mind. Yet, when they had completed the circuit of the glass-houses and grounds, he courteously excused him from further attendance. "We have seen all," he said, "and I fear we have tired you more than we should. We will linger and rest awhile in the cooler galleries, but to ask you to remain longer would be an imposition upon one whose time is surely of more value than ours."

The old gentleman, who had better wits than his appearance disclosed, heard this in some doubt of whether he were being treated as courteously as the suave words would suggest, but he had no doubt of what he should do. He took his leave, ceremoniously to all, and with real cordiality to Dr. Dalston, in whom he had recognised a brother scientist, who brought some knowledge and much more alert perception to what he saw.

When the director had gone, the four delegates of Baratá were alone, except for an occasional garden attendant passing about, and the discreetly watchful Bioli police who kept the little party in sight without obtruding too closely upon them.

The gardens had not been officially closed, but there had been a plain warning in the morning *Gazette* that visitors during the afternoon would be scrutinised with a special care, which was a hint not lightly to be ignored, and, in fact, those who did present themselves at the turnstile gates were subjected to an inquisition from which they usually turned or were turned away.

Such gardens in Central America have an opposite difficulty from that which must be faced in more temperate lands. They do not require heat, though humidity must be provided. But they do need artificial coolness for plants which come from northern or southern zones, or from the mountains of their own lands.

There was a circular cooled house for such specimens, built with a wide, roofed, vine-hung balcony sweeping round it on which it was pleasant to linger, for a current of tempered air blew continually outward from the ventilators, and even when the sun declined, as it did now, it gave more heat to a heavy windless atmosphere than men were anxious to feel.

The sweep of the balcony was broken in places by walls which rose to the roof and came forward to within three feet of the balustrade which looked down on the open gardens.

Conradi passed round one of these walls, but was no more than a moment away. As he came back, Enrico bent to read the name of a trailing plant with great black-splashed purple flowers, their petals shaped like a giant butterfly's wings, and in that instant Conradi signed with his hand to the two others to go round the partitioning wall. "There is a seat," he said, in a low but casual tone, "at the back, where you will be safe. I will join you there."

They strolled round at once, though with no appearance of haste, so that they could not see how long Enrico bent over the labelled plant, or what Conradi might do.

There was a short minute during which they reached the seat which Conradi had mentioned. They heard nothing, and he did not join them, as they had anticipated that he would do.

Serati said: "I have been told that his favourite method is to slip the bomb into his victim's pocket, it being so made that it will explode when he becomes conscious of it, and puts his hand to feel what is there. But it gives Conradi the needed minutes to get away. Any moment now he will come scuttling round like a frightened coney, and then we shall hear the bang."

He smiled slightly, feeling the interest of the event to be some compensation for any material disappointments which might be involved in Dr. Dalston's death.

He reached the seat as he spoke, and noticed a small, silver-mounted, sandalwood box, no larger than a snuff-box, lying upon it.

"Someone," he said, "will be missing this," picking it up idly for closer inspection, but he found that he had grasped something from which it would be less easy to part. A glutinous substance upon the side of the little box held his finger to it.

"The sun's heat," he said, "has melted it."

"The sun's heat," Señor Philipo thought, "in this shadowed place? Stop! Don't pull it!" he cried. His voice was shrill with fear. For one half-second he knew the terror of coming death, which lacked time to enter his companion's mind, for, at the slight wrench, the bomb burst, as it had been constructed to do.

Andreas Conradi had obeyed the instructions of President Cortéz, which had not changed, as he had not thought that they would.

CHAPTER TWENTY-ONE

THE EFFECTS OF A GOOD BOMB

THERE could be no doubt that Conradi made a good bomb. It burst with a deafening sound in that low-roofed balcony, and an acrid stench met Conradi as he advanced, with an exclamation of horrified surprise, to investigate what had occurred. Enrico, with greater caution, but greater courage also, being in ignorance of what it might mean, followed a pace behind.

They came on an air that was still thick with smoke, and their first sight was the torn and blackened vines that had hung down from the roof to the balustrade; and then, looking down, they saw Señor Philipo.

With great presence of mind, he had been already flinging himself to the ground as the bomb burst, but it had been of no advantage to him. The inner shell of the bomb had been so constructed that it would break into a score of needle-sharp brittle fragments, and one of these, by what may be considered an evil chance, had pierced the side of his throat, inflicting a wound which must have been fatal alone, but, besides that, the force of the explosion had thrown his half-fallen body against the balustrade with a force which had split his skull.

He had been so cast that he sat on the ground with his back to the balustrade, his legs spread widely apart, and his head hanging forward, as though in a vain effort to stay the tide of out-pulsing blood. His body twitched a little, as though still protesting against the violence which had flung it about, but, in spite of that, it might not be far wrong to say that he was already dead.

Conradi bent over him, as though in an attempt to do something for one who was clearly beyond human aid, but he had a more reasonable purpose than that. He was aware, without turning his head, that Enrico had passed him now through the clearing smoke (which the current of ventilation air carried rapidly away) looking at Señor Serati's even less sightly remains, and, in that instant, he drew from the breast-pocket of the dead man the wallet into which he had seen him put the document which he had signed a few hours before.

In the next second his opportunity would have gone, for there was an inrush of the military police, jostling, cursing, exclaiming, reduced to half-articulate volubility by the consternation of the event.

A black-browed half-breed, who had fixed his bayonet as he ran, exclaimed, "They may have another! Let us reach them before they throw." Enrico, told to hold up his hands, and failing to comply with the alacrity which is better understood in the New World than the Old, saw the bayonet point at his waistcoat button, but was saved from the alternatives of violence or ignominy by Conradi's vigorous and denunciatory protests, he taking easy control of a scene which may have had no great novelty for him.

The next moment an officer arrived who took charge with a cooler and more intelligent authority. He did not offer any supplementary insult to the survivors of the little party of his country's guests, but he had the wit to say: "Excellency, it is a sad sight. Who could have supposed that they would wish to destroy themselves in such a manner as this?"

"They have not destroyed themselves," Enrico replied sharply. "They were not men of a kind who would do that. They have been killed in a manner of which you may know more than I."

The officer politely ignored the implication of this remark. He said: "Señors, there were none here but yourselves. We are all witnesses of that. We have kept a most close watch."

Enrico saw that another implication had been made, less clumsily than his own. It was as though the officer had said: "There were none here but yourselves. When I suggest that they died by their own hands, I speak the words of a friend. For, otherwise, by what hands but yours could it have been? Do you resent that I open a gate for your own release?"

But Enrico was in no mind to accept such a hint, or to admit that he had any need to be concerned for his own defence. He knew himself to be utterly innocent, and the thought that Conradi might be less so did not enter his mind. He said: "I do not know who was here, and who not. Nor can I tell that what you know and what you say to me are the same thing.

"What I know is that my friends are dead, as I suppose we should all have been had not I, and Señor Conradi here, lingered behind. It is a bomb, by a simple guess, that was meant for me.

"And as to no one being there, would you expect them to stay till the explosion occurred?"

The officer, who had a sensitive Latin pride, flushed when he heard his own veracity so rudely challenged, but he had sufficient sense of the gravity of the position, and the censure to which he might be himself exposed, not to make an angry reply.

He would have sworn, three minutes before, that the building contained no living man but the four whom it had been his duty to guard, and that the balcony had been dear of anything which should not be there. But the explosion had been a fact. It was beyond denial now, and its consequences could not be undone.

"Señor," he said, with some dignity, "I can but say what I saw—or what I did not see. But the truth is seldom too hard to find."

"Then I hope you may find it on this occasion. I am going back to the Legation now. I suppose you will lose no time in acquainting President Gómez with what has occurred."

"Señor, he will be promptly informed, and will without doubt express to you and to your President the sorrow for this mischance which all Bioli will feel. You will permit me to send a guard to assure your safety to your own door?"

"No, I would prefer not."

The officer bowed in silence, as though accepting this decision, though he flushed again at the implication which it conveyed.

Enrico, returning to the Legation in a car which had held four, and now had Conradi for his sole and very silent companion, reflected that the officer had shown himself to be a capable, and he thought him to be, an honest man. He was not surprised to observe a police-car following closely upon his trail.

But his mind was most concerned with the puzzle of the tragedy which had occurred, and that he should prove capable of dealing with it as the obligations of his office required.

The men themselves had not been of a congeniality to rouse him to much regret at their sudden ends, and his professional experiences had familiarised him to such sights as that on which he had gazed.

He was indignant at an outrage so gross, and which seemed to have the complexion of a political crime rather than one of private vengeance. But his indignation would have been more had he been puzzled less. It seemed such a purposeless—even an inexplicable—crime.

The true solution not entering his mind even as a fantastic possibility, he was inevitably led to consider President Gómez as the instigator of the event. He knew enough of the politics of Bioli to be of a decided opinion that such assassination would not be arranged without the knowledge and approval of the President, in whom all authority centred. But what motive could he have?

He had planned war, as the cargo of the *Billy Winch* abundantly testified. Was it possible that it was a course which he still preferred, and that he had chosen this drastic method of ending peaceful negotiations? It was at least a possible explanation.

But he could not avoid observing that President Gómez could hardly have selected his victims. If he had ordered a bomb to be so placed that they would stumble upon it, while appearing to be securely alone, he must at least have contemplated the possibility—probably expected—that the whole party would perish, he himself included.

Evidently the fact that he had married Juliana the day before had not been a sufficient argument for his preservation. Suddenly—sickeningly—the thought came that it might, on the contrary, be the reason for what had occurred. Suppose that President Gómez, determined to bring the differences between the two countries to the decision of war, or distrustful of the good faith of the proposals which were being made, had felt himself so embarrassed thereby that when he also had to face the fact that his daughter had become the bride of the Envoy of Baratá, or perhaps having been secretly infuriated by the suggestion that the *Billy Winch* might be turned aside, he had resolved on that drastic method of removal of the man who complicated or spoiled his plans?

Enrico strove to put so foul a doubt from his mind. But the assassinations were fact. It was a fact also—at least to him—that whoever placed that bomb must have expected, if not hoped, that it would lead to his own death. He remembered the reticent manner with which President Gómez had received the confidences which he had thrust upon him, and the doubt grew.

And he had supposed that he would be taking up his own residence in the Palazzo within the next hour! What would the President do when he heard that the bomb had failed to reach the one at whom it had been primarily aimed? What cunning pit might be dug, what secret violence contrived, to destroy him now? What, above all, would Juliana do? What restraint might be put upon her?

At the best, if his immunity as an envoy should be respected, which was much to hope after what had just occurred, he saw himself returning to Baratá, and divided from his just-won bride by the outbreak of bitter war.

His mind disturbed by these thoughts, he scarcely listened when, immediately after he had regained the Legation, Conradi handed him Señor Philipo's wallet. He had abstracted the document which he sought, and the major portion of a surprisingly large sum of money which it contained. But he had been too prudent to take the whole amount, or to retain the wallet.

"I had just time," he said, "to remove this from Señor Philipo's pocket before the police arrived. I thought it might contain documents which should not be seen by the enemies of Baratá. But it should be in your charge, and for your examination, rather than mine."

Absent-mindedly, Enrico took it, and approved what had been done.

Feeling that he could have no peace till he had resolved the dreadful doubt that was on his mind, he attempted to ring up President Gómez, and was rebuffed with the information that the President's line was likely to be engaged for some time. He tried to get through to San Cristóval, and was informed that President Cortéz was similarly occupied. He concluded correctly that they were talking to one another. Only Juliana remained. With a hand that, to his own annoyance, trembled with anxiety, he lifted the receiver again and asked to be put through to her.

CHAPTER TWENTY-FIVE

CAPTAIN PÉREZ MAKES A MISTAKE

THE mistake which Captain Pérez made is one for which he can hardly be blamed. The name and person of Señor Philipo had long been familiar to him as those of the Envoy of Baratá. He was more concerned with the efficient discharge of his own semi-military duties than with the personnel of the various foreign legations in San Sebastián.

When he had first seen the little party for whose safety he would be responsible, and had observed Señor Philipo among them, he had naturally assumed that he was still the official representative of Baratá. It was a mistake which more than one around him could have corrected, but why should it occur to them that he was less accurately informed than themselves, or that it was a point on which it was material that he should be instructed? When he had come upon the dying man, he had recognised Señor Philipo, and did not doubt that the assassination had been aimed at—and reached—the Envoy himself, and it was that fact, with all its political significances, rather than the individual, which had impressed his competent mind.

As to the second death—the fate of Señor Serati, of whose status in his own country he did not know, seemed to him a mere detail in its comparative unimportance. He scarcely looked at a man who had, in fact, become difficult to identify, even in a better light than that in which he was distributed over the floor.

Consequently, when he telephoned to President Gómez, which he did very promptly, judging it to be an event on which the President would wish to have the earliest and most direct information, he said that a bomb must have been concealed on the balcony which had proved fatal to the Envoy of Baratá and one of his suite. He was actually corrected by a subordinate standing by, who said: "No, it was Señor Philipo," at which he added, without understanding the point of the correction, the name of the dead man, but the President took this to be that of the "member of the suite" whose death he had already mentioned. He did not doubt that Dr. Dalston was dead.

President Gómez had not gained the dangerous eminence which he now occupied, and which he had held for fifteen turbulent years, without having learned to face an unexpected emergency in a prompt and resolute mood. He knew it to be a vital condition of his security that he should make the right guess when faced by a sudden doubt, and that, having made it, he should act upon it without further hesitation. Now he saw himself to be faced with both national and domestic crises of the first magnitude, one of which was (he supposed) without remedy, and the other suggested an extremity of danger for the state he ruled.

He had an affection for Juliana of the strength of which he was himself hardly aware, and he was now stirred by contending passions of sorrow for what appeared to be the irreparable grief which must close the romance of her one-day marriage, and fierce anger against whoever had been responsible for the crime.

In considering who its author might be, he could not fall into the same error as Enrico, for he knew himself to be innocent; nor could he think that anyone in Bioli would, for political reasons, without his knowledge, contrive so purposeless an assassination.

He considered the explanation of private vengeance. But what enemies in Bioli was it likely that Dr. Dalston would have made, occupied as he had been?

Could it be the work of some jealous rival for Juliana's affections? It was a motive, and a method of vengeance, which would appear more probable to a Latin than an English mind, but it was unconvincing here.

He was not aware that Juliana had indulged in anything beyond the lightest and most innocent of flirtations since she had returned to San Sebastián. Serious entanglement he was sure that there had not been. And, besides, the method of the crime itself discounted this possibility. It must have entailed forethought and planning, or resources which were not commonly available to a private citizen, even in Bioli or Baratá. Even in San Sebastián bombs of reliable quality are not openly sold!

A private rival would have been a thousand times more likely to hire such an assassin as would have used a knife in the back, or a shot from a passing car.

From these negative conclusions, President Gómez went on to consider whether Dr. Dalston's destruction might not be the act of his own friends. He had observed that there was little cordiality between him and the other members of the delegation. Might not his efforts during the last twenty-four hours to take control, and establish a real, for what might have been intended to be no more than a semblance of peace, have decided them that he had become a nuisance too great to be longer endured?

This seemed a more feasible explanation. They might have the resources which the occasion required, and it would be natural for them to contrive it in such a way that it would appear to be Bioli's crime, with all the sinister political constructions which might be placed upon it. He saw difficulty in the fact that the victim had declared his purpose of investing capital in Baratá, and it is not a usual Latin-American custom to assassinate people with such admirable intentions before they have had time to instruct their bankers in the right way. But was it possible that Dr. Dalston had been more reticent to his uncongenial colleagues than to himself, and that they had killed the goose in ignorance of the golden eggs which it had been about to lay?

But even accepting that possibility, which was discounted by the telephone conversation he had overheard earlier in the day, he went on to reflect that so drastic a method of removing Baratá's accredited envoy would not have been employed by his colleagues without their President's authority. Yet what adequate motive could he have for such violent interference with the course of negotiations he had started himself? Searching for an answer to this riddle, the President's agile mind came to the neighbourhood of the truth as he asked himself—*what, indeed, unless it were to embroil Bioli with Baratá?*

With the thought, his resolution was formed. He would be the one to acquaint President Cortéz with the calamity of his envoy's death, and would be able to observe his first reactions thereto. Before Enrico's swift-moving car had arrived at his own door, President Gómez had rung up the Postmaster-General, ascertained that no one had been in communication with San Cristóval during the last hour, and that neither by telephonic nor telegraphic channels had news of the tragedy been sent abroad, given emphatic instructions that no such messages were to be allowed except by his own permission, and ordered that President Cortéz should be rung up and requested to speak to him on a matter of the utmost urgency. He did not suppose that he would be met in an attitude of simple candour. It would either be a tale as startling to his hearer as to himself, or a battle of wits in which he had some confidence in his own capacity.

President Cortéz was, as we know, well prepared to hear the echoed noise of that bursting bomb. He had decided upon the degree of surprise which it would be natural, and the extremity of indignation which it would be expedient to show, in conformity with plans which had been radically modified during the last few hours. Through the years that he had held the dangerous but lucrative position of President of Baratá, he had rarely had a settled policy which went beyond the end of the current month. He had held his place by a personal magnetism and power of dominating oratory which could sway to his mood an excitable Latin crowd, a ruthless removal of potential enemies or too powerful friends, and an expert opportunism which swung quick yards round to the changing winds.

The startling information regarding Dr. Dalston's power and intentions which he had received from Señor Philipo a few hours before had not been lightly regarded, for he knew the ex-envoy to be a man of discreet judgment, and not one who would say more than the facts supported. He had been instant in cabling to verify the suggestion that Dr. Dalston might have the power to divert the course of the *Billy Winch*, and having been assured of this, he had directed his mind to consideration of two opposite modifications of his previous plans.

He was not troubled by the fear of destroying a possible bene-factor of Baratá, which had agitated the minds of Señors Philipo and Serati, for the sufficient reason that that had never—beyond the length of one transient hour—been his intention.

Almost instantly, he had decided to send the two with whom the plan had originated, as colleagues for Dr. Dalston, and as sacrificial substitutes whom he felt it would be easy to spare. Consequently, he was the less concerned with the indiscretion of the telephone con-versations which had been thrust upon him during the morning. Had he anticipated that they would be followed by Dr. Dalston's assassi-nation, there had been words spoken, however vague, which he would have regarded as indiscreet. But could it be supposed that the delegates who had been telephoning to him had been alluding to the contingency of their own deaths? The idea would be radically ab-surd!

He had not doubted that Conradi would carry out, with his usual efficiency, the assassinations he had undertaken; and he had consid-ered the possibility of making that the cause of war which he had first intended, with the additional advantage of obtaining Dr. Dal-ston's assistance to divert the *Billy Winch's* cargo to a quayside of Baratá; and, oppositely, of allowing the negotiations to lead up to a genuine peace, such as would provide a healthy atmosphere for the reception of the Englishman's substantial loans. With the liberal percentage of such investments which, by open or subterranean channels, he anticipated receiving, added to the considerable wealth which he had already accumulated, he seriously considered the ex-pediency of retiring from his present dangerous eminence, to such a villa in Southern Europe as is suitable to the dignity of that minority of the ex-presidents of South and Central America who end their careers without experiencing a firing-squad, or an assassin's knife, or the monotony of a prison cell.

He saw that neither plan was free from difficulties. Dr. Dal-ston's co-operation was essential to the full success of the first, and the second involved reconciling his own people to a treaty by which they would surrender rights to which they had been taught to attach a patriotic importance, and from which the bulk of the country's revenue was derived.

But he did not consider either alternative impossible of successful accomplishment. Between them, after some hesitation, he had decided that he preferred the second. He saw that to forgive Bioli for the monstrous outrage for which it would be responsible would be a gesture to win the world's sympathy to himself, and the subsequent offer of very modified concessions would be very difficult for President Gómez to refuse. Even though he might not succeed in preventing the cargo of munitions reaching San Luíz harbour, the fact of the assassinations, added to his willingness to make concessions to Bioli's claims, would make it very difficult for that country to begin an unprovoked war, for the time, at least. And, meanwhile, Dr. Dalston's £200,000 would be secured!

Having come to this sound and magnanimous decision, President Cortéz waited for the news which he expected at any moment to hear. He did not, of course, know that Conradi had planned to execute his purpose in the Garden of Many Plants, but he knew that he had instructed him to be expeditious in what he did. The passing days had now brought the *Billy Winch* very near to its destination. Within a few days, if the seas were smooth, and Dr. Dalston did not interfere, it might be unloading its weapons of death on San Luíz quay. President Cortéz adjusted his mind for the reception of a telephone call which he felt certain would soon be made.

CHAPTER TWENTY-SIX

THE TELEPHONE
CONVERSATION OF THE TWO PRESIDENTS

"THAT you, Gómez?" President Cortéz began, before his brother president could open the unpleasant tale that he had to tell. "I have just passed the draft provisions of the proposed treaty, in a form which—"

There was certainly nothing in the affability of his voice to suggest that he was expecting to hear of his envoy's murder, but it was not a matter that could be deferred.

President Gómez interrupted with: "Thanks, but it wasn't about that I was ringing you up. I'm very sorry to have to tell you that a tragic affair occurred this afternoon. I haven't any details yet. I only heard of it a few minutes ago. But there was an explosion of some kind in the Garden of Many Plants while the members of your delegation were visiting there, and I am sorry to say that there have been two deaths among them in consequence." President Cortéz answered in a voice which had become grave and cold: "*Explosion?* That is a vague and ominous word. Are you informing me that members of my delegation have been assassinated in your public gardens?"

"No. It would be an improbable—indeed, an inexplicable— crime, if such a thing had occurred. You will agree that there are potentialities of accident to be probed. There is the possibility of the two unfortunate gentlemen having fallen victims to a vengeance intended for others. There is the possibility of suicide, or of the premature explosion of a bomb in their own possession.

"I do not, of course," he hastened to add, for he had heard an exclamation at the other end of the wire which he did not like, "put any of these possibilities forward even as a theory of what has occurred. I only say that in a matter of such gravity, it is important to preserve open minds until the full facts can be ascertained. But I felt it my duty to inform you immediately, before there has been time to do so; and to express my profound regret that such an event should have occurred, from whatever cause, at a time when these gentlemen were officially accredited here."

The voice of President Cortéz still had a steel-like quality as he replied, but his words were better than his auditor had expected to hear: "You may accept my assurance that I shall consider the facts with an open mind, and that I should regret as much as yourself any disturbance of the relations of our respective countries, at a time when we had appeared to be on the point of removing all outstanding differences."

"It is the most that I could expect you to say. I will communicate with you again in the next hour, and you can rest assured that the fullest information will be placed before you, and that no effort will be spared by us to ascertain the true facts, and to do whatever justice they may require."

"I cannot ask," President Cortéz replied, in an almost placable voice, "at this stage, for a fuller assurance than that; and you, on your part, will recognise that I can do no more than reserve my judgment. But can you give me the names of those who have been the victims of this—incident—or have they not yet come to your knowledge?"

It was a question which might naturally have been asked at an earlier moment, but the delicacy with which President Gómez had commenced to break the news of the event, and the fact that the ruler of Baratá believed himself to be already acquainted with the victims' names, had combined to defer it.

"I regret that it was Doctor Dalston and Señor Philipo who—"

"*Doctor Dalston?*"

"Yes. I understood that the two gentlemen had gone somewhat in advance of their companions, and had actually turned a corner, so that they were unobserved by any others, when the explosion occurred. It is that fact, in particular, which renders it so difficult even to theorise as to what may have happened."

It was during this part of the conversation that President Gómez observed that Juliana had entered the room. It was one which was strictly private to himself, and guarded by a secretary who, in the anteroom which was its only approach, was now occupied in listening in and recording the conversation. But Juliana was a privileged visitor, though she would not be likely to intrude without particular reason, which she felt that she now had.

Her father concluded from her demeanour that she was unaware of the tragic death of the man she had married on the previous day, and he would have chosen a less abrupt and indirect method of informing her of it, but how could he refuse to answer the question of President Cortéz on such a ground?

Now the effects of the announcement were unexpected upon both his auditors. Juliana heard the news of her lover's death with no more than a puzzled frown which changed to a look suggestive rather of amusement than grief. President Cortéz, after the pause of consternation which had given time for explanation of how the tragedy had occurred, said curtly: "You tell me that my envoy is dead? It is an outrage for which I must hold Bioli to the strictest account. Following, as it does, an inexplicable tragedy during the night, in which Señor Serati's secretary was killed, you cannot expect that I shall allow him to risk his life longer in such conditions. I feel that I must recall any members of the delegation who may remain alive. You will expect that they will leave Bioli tomorrow."

The words were ominous enough, but they were spoken in the tone of an infuriated man. President Gómez recognised that the names of the victims had altered the atmosphere of the conversation, so that he was suddenly faced with what might mean no less than a declaration of war, at an earlier day than, if it must come at all, he would have preferred it to be. He saw it to have some explanation, though less than one of strict logic, if President Cortéz had been assuming that the victims had been two subordinate members of Dr. Dalston's suite (and such as he would not be over reluctant to lose?).

With better logic, though contrary to the fact, it appeared to make it more probable that the President of Baratá was innocent of provoking this most puzzling crime.

Blaming himself for having, as he thought, caused misunderstanding by an unfortunate reticence, and knowing himself as blameless as he now supposed his brother president to be, his mind searched for any argument he could offer, sufficient to bring conviction of his own innocence of the crime.

"I do not say," he replied temperately, "that you would not be justified in regarding the matter in such a light, though I feel assured that fuller information must place a different construction upon it; but you will, I am sure, understand that it is an event as tragic to ourselves as to you, when I tell you that it was only yesterday that my daughter was married to Doctor Dalston."

It was a second thing which President Cortéz certainly had not expected to hear, and as he paused again to adjust his mind to this startling fact, he heard something further which was not intended for him. Faintly, a girl's voice asked, in a half-laughing, half-derisive voice: "Have you been telling someone that Enrico is dead?" Then President Gómez said clearly: "Will you pardon me for one moment only?" and it became obvious that the receiver was covered. President Gómez looked up to say, with the gravity which the announcement required: "There has been a serious accident. I am afraid."

"I know all about that. I was talking to Enrico on my own phone less than two minutes ago. He's coming straight here. I've told him it's the only safe place to be."

"Then did he tell you who was killed? Or is the whole thing a hoax?"

"Serati and Philipo were killed, and I shouldn't think they are much loss, though I suppose, if it's Cortéz you're having that loving chat with, you'd better not say so. It looks as though he did it himself more likely than not. But I told Enrico he shouldn't stay with that gang for another hour, even if you hadn't invited him here before this blow-up occurred."

"And he is content to come?"

"Well, I should hope he is!"

"You have done the best thing you could. You may have saved us from war."

Her father, feeling an immense relief on more counts than one, removed his covering hand from the instrument. The conversation had taken more than the moment for which he had asked, but it was not surprising that President Cortéz was still there.

"I am pleased to be able to tell you that my first information was incorrect. Doctor Dalston is alive and unhurt. I am, however, sorry to say that there appears to have been no error regarding the number of the victims. Señors Philipo and Serati, according to the latest information, were killed."

President Cortéz heard that for which his mind had been already prepared, but he had had time to observe the inexpediency of appearing to fluctuate in the degree of his indignation as the names of the victims changed. Now he said only: "Then, as my envoy still lives, I must prefer to receive a report from him, after which I may speak to you again."

"It is a procedure to which I cannot object, and you may like to know that you will be able to get Doctor Dalston on the telephone at the Palazzo here with me, within the next hour. We have invited him here, so that his security may be guarded equally with my own."

"He has accepted that invitation?"

"Yes, so I have just heard from my daughter."

"Perhaps you will ask him to await a further communication from me when he arrives?"

"Yes, you can depend upon that."

President Cortéz rang off.

CHAPTER TWENTY-SEVEN

CONRADI KNOWS NOTHING OF BOMBS

ENRICO did not arrive at the Palazzo within an hour. It was much longer than that.

He had yielded to the urgency of Juliana's voice in consenting to go there in spite—she would have said all the more because—of what had occurred. She was one whom, while her voice was at his ear, he was unable to doubt. And he felt that, if she were false, there was little value for him in the life which he would risk under her father's roof. But of President Gómez he was less sure.

Yet Juliana's vividly expressed confidence in her father's good faith, and equally emphatic accusation of the President of Baratá, could not fail to have its effect upon the confusion of his own mind. That one or other of the two Presidents had aimed at his own death was a natural conclusion for him to reach. Having missed, was it not likely that he would strike again? He felt that he had had enough of the political methods of Bioli and Baratá.

He could not regret that he had come, when his thought turned, as it was frequent to do, to the bride whom he had won. But that was a thought which made life dearer than it had been before, and to be less wantonly risked. As a choice of perils, he would go to the Palazzo tonight. He would trust himself to Juliana's arms. Thinking of how he had found Pedro crouching outside his bedroom door during the last night—which Juliana had not failed to recall to his mind—judgment supported inclination in that decision. He supposed the events to be more closely allied than, in fact, they were. Was it not possible that his going out during the night, and the fortunate blow which had sent Pedro to sudden death, had frustrated some plot which had been designed against him, and caused that to be substituted by the bomb in the Garden of Many Plants? It seemed likely; though there were difficulties in formulating a theory of what had saved his life and occasioned the deaths of his two colleagues. But, suppose there had been premature explosion of a bomb which had been intended for him?

It was a theory which supported Juliana's confident opinion, and exonerated her father, and to that extent it was what he would be glad to believe. But, be it as it might, it did not alter his decision that he had had sufficient experience of the countries of his own and his mother's births.

He no longer thought of establishing a peace founded on his own influence and wealth. He recognised the argument of the bomb to be one to which there is no reply. He did not think of diverting the course of the *Billy Winch*. He had a better use for it than that.

In a week's time, more or less, it would cast anchor in San Luíz harbour, and when it did so, he meant to be there. He did not mean to return to England alone. It would be a test of Juliana's love, and of her loyalty, in which he did not think she would fail.

Tonight, he would put it to her, and stake all on her devotion to him. If she should prove unequal to such a test—well, she was not the first woman who had failed to answer the call of love, nor he the first man who had been betrayed! But he had a much better hope.

He went to his own room, and began to pack such things as he would require, or was unwilling to leave, and as he did so the question rose in his mind, would there be any opposition to his removing to the Palazzo from those who still remained alive within the Legation walls?

It seemed an absurd idea, they being men whose duty was to take orders from him, but he was in a mood to doubt all.

There was Hernández. He had not been friendly to him. Rather, he had favoured Señor Philipo, though perhaps rather through fear than love. But it was certain that any loyalty he might have had for the ex-envoy had not been potent to save his life. On the whole, he was disposed to put suspicion of him aside. A routine clerk, whose first concern would be to keep the position he had, and who would neither be chosen nor proffer himself for complicity in a murderous plot. Indeed, the manner in which he had received the news of what had occurred ruled him out, unless he were a consummate actor, which Enrico was not inclined to believe.

Andreas Conradi remained. A dark inscrutable man. Enrico considered him, and encountered a mask that he could not pierce. He was an accountant. A man of figures. A customs clerk. The disguise, if such it were, was good, because it was of a genuine kind. But he was a man whom it was as easy to distrust as it was hard to know.

Considering him, and reconstructing the event in which they had been so near their companions' deaths, a sudden memory came. Disregarded, scarcely observed at the time, having no apparent importance then, he was yet sure that Conradi had preceded the other two round that fatal corner, and returned before they went to encounter death. Why bad he done that? To inspect plants? As they had wandered about, it had become evident that Conradi knew little of the flora of the American continent, and, if possible, cared even less.

It was far short of proof, but it was evidence sinister enough to decide him to probe the fact in a bold way. He sought Conradi, and put a blunt question to him, such as an innocent man might resent and a guilty one might not receive with any greater pleasure. But, perhaps, differently.

"Conradi," he asked, "why did you place that bomb?"

Conradi met the question with a straight stare. He had been annoyed before that President Cortéz should have allowed the two men who were now dead to know of the profession in which he secretly specialised. It made it at least possible that he had given the same confidence to the Envoy whom he had selected to live. But those men were dead. Conradi had no intention of making the throwing of bombs a subject of ordinary conversation with all he met. He said, with a stubborn scowl: "I know nothing of bombs." He added, thinking that it must be a relevant consideration to any sensible man: "They were no friends to you. It is your enemies who have died."

It was the discordance of English and Latin ideals and temperaments which, as he did not understand it, he could not be expected to meet. To Enrico, he had exposed at once his own guilt, and a character which it was natural to loathe.

"Had you been instructed to do so," he asked curiously, "you would as willingly have placed it for me?"

"Excellency, I know nothing of bombs. But we are in the service of Baratá."

Enrico felt that he had been answered again, in ambiguous but still unmistakable words. From that moment, he exonerated President Gómez from any responsibility for the incident of the afternoon, though he remained in some doubt of whether his methods might not have some similarity, if a like occasion should be his. The Palazzo became a more desirable refuge, the open leaving of the Legation a more hazardous adventure. He was, in fact, in no danger at all. He had good reason for fear.

Considering that possessions are less than life, and that the unexpected course may be the safer when surrounded by treacherous foes, he neither took luggage nor ordered his car. He walked out into the streets which were now crowded in the cool of the evening hour, and proceeded to the Palazzo on foot. He was aware, though he would not appear to notice, that two policemen followed closely behind him, and reasonably concluded that their intentions had not been unfriendly when he arrived safely at the main entrance of the Palazzo and was received with solicitous courtesy by the officials at its guarded doors.

CHAPTER TWENTY-EIGHT

PRESIDENT CORTÉZ IS NOT PLEASED

PRESIDENT CORTÉZ, having concluded his conversation with the ruler of the neighbour republic, considered his difficulties, and as be considered them, they did not decrease.

Señors Serati and Philipo were dead. He was glad of that. The first had become difficult to satisfy or control, having formed the opinion that he was indispensable to the President's safety, which was not a healthy idea for such a man to have. The second was commonly reputed to have considered himself competent to succeed to the presidential dignity, if at any time its existing holder should find the cares of office too heavy to be longer sustained, or should meet with one of those accidents to which presidents are so peculiarly liable when other men are waiting to take their places.

Both of them were much better dead; and they had died in such a way that suspicion would more naturally fall upon the ruler of Bioli than the one who had been actually responsible for their abrupt departures. That was good, and President Cortéz did well to observe it with all the satisfaction it deserved, for it was about all the good that he was able to see.

Earlier in the day, he had thought the news of Dr. Dalston's influence and intentions had an excellent sound. Even ten minutes ago, he had been roused to furious anger by the belief that he had been killed. But he did not know then that he had become the son-in-law of Bioli's President. He had not heard that he was leaving the Legation of Baratá, preferring the protection of the Palazzo's walls.

Not knowing that he had previously received and accepted an invitation to do this, the fact appeared to be more significant than it actually was. Did it mean that Baratá's envoy was definitely changing sides? That the sound of that disastrous bomb had decided him to place himself and his resources at the service of the President whose daughter had become his bride? It had a very probable appearance.

And, if so, what advantage was it that he could control the course of the *Billy Winch*? Obviously, none. Or that he had wealth which he was prepared to use in whatever cause he might make his own? Less than none. For it might now be used exclusively for Bioli, and particularly so if the two countries should be at war, so that he must choose an exclusive side.

Bioli's army was small. But if the resources of its treasury should be swelled with an extra quarter of a million pounds, those ranks would be doubled within a week. Soldiers in every country like to be paid, and those of Central America no less because the normal probabilities are not great.

Still, this was no more than surmise. Dr. Dalston might still be loyal to Baratá. Even if he were conscious of a divided allegiance, he might still hope to promote peace between the two countries by means of the treaty which he had been negotiating. It might still be possible to persuade him to divert the course of the *Billy Winch*. Possible, but how? A telephone conversation was the obvious means of giving such instructions. But it was obviously impossible also. Even had Dr. Dalston been of an assured loyalty, and had there been a fuller understanding with him, it would have been difficult to discuss the subject in so cryptic a manner that it could not be understood by those who would be certainly listening in. And the mere suspicion would be enough to cause President Gómez to take any necessary steps, however drastic, to avert such a catastrophe. Even if that difficulty should be overcome, how could a radio message to the *Billy Winch* pass the certain censorship to which it would be subjected in the Bioli post office?

Had there been more time, it would have been the obvious course to recall Baratá's envoy and discuss the matter with him in

San Cristóval, from which city a radio could be safely sent. As it was, there could be no more than a small chance that he could return in time, and, meanwhile, the decision of peace or war must be taken, or the whole purpose of forcing a quarrel before the cargo could be discharged would be gone.

Yet, even so, a slender chance must be seized if it be the only one that there is; and President Gómez had been told already that Baratá's envoy would be recalled. He paused in his anxious thoughts to order that the presidential train should be dispatched instantly at full steam to San Sebastián, to be placed at Dr. Dalston's disposal there.

Resuming his reflections, he saw that there was no occasion for haste in regard to a conversation which must take place in President Gómez's palace. There might even be advantage in some delay. He decided to first make public the tale of the shocking deaths of two of Baratá's most prominent and respected citizens while on a mission of peace and goodwill to the country in which they died. He gave orders to close the frontier, and for his little army to move toward it, in readiness for an invasion on which he might decide during the next day. That was to be public news for the world to know. It was a gesture of indignation, which neutral opinion could hardly fail to approve. It demonstrated the shock with which the news of the assassinations had been received. If he should afterwards take a more magnanimous attitude, would he not earn the admiration of the whole world, as one who, under provocation, had refused to plunge the two countries into the miseries of a modern war?

Giving the mature consideration to these complicated problems which they surely required, and feeling that there was no real loss of time while the presidential train puffed and clanked up the precipitous estuary side, President Cortéz delayed to call up Dr. Dalston until a late hour in the evening.

Meanwhile, Dr. Dalston, walking through the cool crowded streets, with the ambiguous police escort at his back, had also had time for further reflections, which led him to modify some of his earlier conclusions. He had already dismissed his first suspicions that President Gómez had sought his life, either as an unwelcome son-in-law, or as one holding a too-dangerous power over the helm of the *Billy Winch*. He had exonerated him from all responsibility for the outrage, whether aimed at himself or others. And he now saw that, so far as he himself was concerned, he must admit the innocence of President Cortéz also. He did not doubt that Conradi had killed those whom his orders required him to do. The executions—if that were the right word for this method of governmental removal!—could therefore have no relation whatever to anything which he had done, or might be intending to do, unless they actually aimed at assisting him in the negotiations he had on hand! He remembered Conradi's remark that it was his enemies who had perished. Suppose President Cortéz had taken this violent and conclusive method of endorsing his own efforts for peace and removing those who would have been secretly active to queer the pitch?

Even that seemed possible! He had to recognise that he was in a world which had standards of conduct different from his own. Perhaps his own standards might be as baffling to them. Perhaps he would be held to observe a low ethical code if he should withdraw now from the high office he had accepted from Baratá? President Cortéz considerately removed those who might have put stones of stumbling before his feet, and the ungrateful Englishman abruptly abandoned the cause he had undertaken at its most critical hour!

But this somewhat fantastic imagination did not deflect him from the purpose which he had formed. Let their or his ethical standards be high or low, they were not the same. Let them go their ways, and he—and Juliana—theirs, and they could not be too far apart. It might be his mother's land, but it was one which she had left at the call of love, as Juliana should be equal to do.

He recognised a more probable (as it was also a truer) theory when he reflected upon the possibility that the double murder had had no better motive than to embroil Bioli with Baratá. But he saw also that such speculations had already led him to do injustice to one President, and to be at least inaccurate in his guess at the other's guilt. It was a doubt which must be confirmed or removed when he should get into communication with President Cortéz, as he must not delay longer to do. He might feel justified in resigning the representation of Baratá in an instant manner, but he must not therefore forget that it was an office which he still held.

With these thoughts, he had come to the Palazzo, and to be shown into the President's private room, where Juliana met him with glad eyes, being relieved from an anxious hour, which had given her time to doubt whether her assurances of loyalty, and urgent entreaty, had prevailed upon him, or whether he had decided that he would not trust himself again to enter the Palazzo doors.

President Gómez greeted him with a friendly gravity. He spoke with deliberation words which he had chosen with care.

"You will not doubt," he said, "my regret for the—tragedy—which has occurred, and which must be in the front of all our minds. But even that must not obstruct the expression of the gratification which I feel that Juliana has made a choice which I so entirely approve. I had planned, as she will have told you, that a public ceremony should follow—shall I say the needless escapade?—of yesterday afternoon. Whether it may be best to keep to that purpose now, or to announce the marriage at once, is one among several matters on which I wish to take counsel with you."

"I am willing that it should be announced in any way and at any time you prefer."

"So I expected that you would say. I should tell you that I have already communicated it to President Cortéz. It is a course which, under normal circumstances, I should not have taken without your previous consent, but it was vital to assure him that I could desire no quarrel either with Baratá or with you. I should tell you also that he expressed an intention of calling you up on your arrival here, which he has not done, though I led him to expect that you would be here at an earlier hour."

"I had intended to ask your permission to speak to him, but if he has said that he will call me up, I will wait for that."

"He also said that he should recall you. He came nearly to threatening war at one time, which he may still mean. But when he was assured that you were unhurt, he spoke in a more moderate way, saying that he would wait your report."

"I had already concluded that, whatever the object of the outrage may have been, it was not aimed at myself."

"I should be glad to have your assurance, beyond that, that you do not hold my Government responsible for it in any way?"

"Speaking between ourselves, I should be glad to say that. But you will allow that I am the Envoy of Baratá. I must not infer more than I certainly know. There is the question of negligence. There may be others which must be raised. Officially, in advance of the enquiry which must obviously be held, I would prefer to say nothing at all."

"But you will use whatever influence you may have to avert war?"

The question brought the fact to Enrico's mind that it was Bioli which had been the first to plot war. Did President Gómez genuinely desire peace now, or merely peace till he should be weaponed for the attack? But he remembered also that those plans were made before there had been any suggestion of composing differences in a better way. Preferences for peace may exist in the minds of unscrupulous men.

But was it a question for him? He had resolved in the last hour that he would break away from the squalid, quasi-criminal politics of these Latin lands, and return to, if not a fairer climate, a cleaner political atmosphere, a more congenial, more comprehensible code.

The instinct of frankness toward one who had become so nearly related to himself, and who seemed to wish to be frank with him, almost led him to express the intention which he had formed, and invite his father-in-law's co-operation in his project of taking Juliana away. After all, he should be glad to see her removed in safety from what might become a much-troubled land. But the instinct of caution which he was learning in that dangerous school, joined to a thought that such a plan should be agreed with Juliana first, kept his lips closed. After all, it would be natural for such a purpose to take shape after he had talked to President Cortéz, and, under normal circumstances, it was a decision which should be communicated to him first.

But the circumstances were far from normal—far, at least, from what was normality to him. His thought before he came to the Palazzo had been rather to slip silently away than to allow his going to be a matter for the consent of these contending plotters. But in the anxious atmosphere of that room, he felt a doubt of what his own honour might require, even some contempt for himself. He must hear what Juliana would say. He recognised that more than once her judgment both of men and events had been sounder than his. It was more nearly her own land.

"Your Excellency," a man-servant at his side was saying, "there is a call for you from San Cristóval. With your permission, I will have it put through to a private room."

He rose, excusing himself, and went to hear what President Cortéz might have to say.

CHAPTER TWENTY-NINE

INSTRUCTIONS FROM PRESIDENT CORTÉZ

"IN an issue of this gravity," President Cortéz said, "I am anxious that nothing should be prejudged, and though I feel it my duty to withdraw the representatives of Baratá from a state which cannot or will not give them the protection to which they are entitled, I am reluctant to take any steps of a punitive character until I have heard your personal report, in addition to that which will doubtless be offered for my consideration by the Bioli government.

"I have therefore sent my own train, on which you and Señor Conradi will return with the utmost expedition to San Cristóval.

"Before leaving, you will inform President Gómez that I have felt it necessary to take certain military measures, in addition to closing the frontier for the next three days; but that, if he be confident that the result of the enquiry will exonerate his own government, he will do well to disregard these measures, as he will have no consequences to apprehend beyond a claim for compensation which, I am sure, he will be prepared to meet. But that any counter-movements of his own troops would be regarded as a declaration of war."

"You do not," Enrico asked, "desire any information from me now as to what occurred?"

"Not by the present medium of communication. I prefer to have your personal report. I will say nothing more now, beyond congratulating you that you were not among the victims, which would have been an irreparable loss to Baratá, and one which I should have been obliged to regard with the utmost gravity. "

"I am satisfied that the bomb was not intended for me."

"It is difficult to see how——," the President began, with a subtle change of tone not pleasant to hear, and then checked himself with: "But you shall tell me all that when we meet," after which he rang off rather abruptly.

Enrico was conscious of the indiscretion of his last words. If there should ever be a place and time for telling President Cortéz what his suspicions were, they were surely not here and now, and it would have been a needless folly to disclose the doubts and disturbance of his own mind.

In fact, President Cortéz had rendered it easy for him to take instructions without committing himself as to what he would do, or expressing any opinion on what had occurred.

What he said had evidently been carefully prepared, and was addressed to intruding listeners as much as himself. In itself, it could not be considered an unreasonable attitude to adopt, if it were allowed that he were innocent of any complicity in the crime. But that was more than Enrico was able to think.

Apart from that, the implication of the message which was to be given to President Gómez was dear. Baratá was to move its military forces, while those of Bioli must remain still, as the one means (if any) of avoiding immediate war. They were to remain still, while President Cortéz made up his mind, at the risk that it might be no more than a bold bluff, and that he might have already resolved upon an invasion which they were to make no preparations to meet. It was much to ask. It was very much to the ears of one who had good reason to think that the double murder had been ordered by the man who now made it the pretext of what he did. Yet, if any prospect of peace remained, it must be through acceptance of these contemptuous terms.

But he saw that the decision was not his. His duty went no further than to communicate to President Gómez the message he had received. Beyond that—and especially if he were intending to retire from the scene, as it were, by the back door—he had neither concern nor control.

Yet when he thought of Bioli as he now saw the position to be, oppressed by excessive tariffs, mocked with false offers, threatened for a crime in which it had no part, indignation urged him to take the part of a country so small and so foully tricked.

But then he remembered that he was still the official representative of Baratá, and his theory of the treachery of its President was conjecture only. Probability, but without proof. While he probed for the falsehood of others, might not the cloak of his own honour be somewhat frayed? Was it not possible that his love for Juliana had warped his judgment? That he had been influenced too much by her view of the characters of those whose cause he had undertaken? Well, he thought (with no consciousness of humour), he must talk it over with her!

He went back to President Gómez, and gave, without comment, the message he had received.

The President (who had heard it already) listened with an expressionless face. He did not appear to question that, if war should come, Enrico would go back, to take his place on the other side. He said only: "I may have something further to say to you before you leave."

The fact was that Juliana had said, while he had still been absent, but after his conversation with San Cristóval had been brought to her father from the tapped wire: "You had better leave Enrico to me," which he had been very willing to do.

The next moment dinner was announced, and during the meal the conversation wandered many ways, but if it came near to the subject in all their minds, there was a common inclination to turn it aside.

Enrico wished to talk to Juliana apart. And he saw that, if the President were not disposed to remain still while his enemies armed, he would not be likely to disclose his purpose, before he must, to the Envoy of Baratá.

It was only as the meal came to its end that President Gómez said: "I can see that it will be necessary to make your marriage known. We must put the idea of a more public ceremony aside. It must be announced that it has already occurred. By your leave, I will have a notice issued in time for it to appear in the morning press."

Enrico said, and meant, that he had no objection at all, but he looked somewhat blank, not instantly seeing how so urgent an occasion arose. Was it, he wondered, with the object of keeping Bioli quiet, if it should be disturbed by rumours of armed forces upon its frontiers, by presenting the marriage as a gesture signifying peace?

"I suppose," the President dryly asked, "if you go tomorrow, you do not intend to leave Juliana behind?"

Enrico became suddenly conscious that the question had not previously entered his mind, doubtless because he had not yet arrived at any settled decision as to what he would do himself. He said hastily: "Is it likely I should? I hope we shall never part while we both live."

President Gómez saw their eyes meet. He observed it to be a point on which they were of one mind. He judged that they were impatient to be alone.

"I am giving you," he said to Enrico, "a room in my own suite, so that your safety may be assured. You will see it is guarded well. If you are disposed to retire, Juliana will show you the way."

Juliana led him to a wing of the palace which was approached by a single corridor. They passed steel shutters and an armed guard.

"President Díaz built this wing," she said. "My father would not have thought it needful, being less hated than he. But it is no harm to sleep safe."

Enrico entered a luxurious room, and looked round with no satisfaction. Last night he had been in another, which he had liked more.

"Your room," he said, "is not here?"

"No. It is the other side of the palace. I am of no importance at all."

"I can come to you?"

"No. It would trouble the guards, who have been told that you must be protected with special care. You must not pass them during the night."

"But I will not be kept apart by such nonsense as that! I am in no danger at all. Can you not find me a room in your own wing? I want to talk to you alone."

"Oh, well, we can do that in the day. You want to talk! But how you look when you sulk. You will always be easy to tease! Enrico, did you think me so cold as that? I will come to you. You will wait no more than a little time."

"You will pass the guard?"

"What of that? They will not think you are in any danger from me. They will enjoy some talk in the night, and tomorrow it will be clear. But you must let me go now, for I shall be the more quickly back."

She struggled from arms that were unwilling to let her go. She passed the guards with a laughing word, smoothing her hair. In the next hour they would see her again. They would understand tomorrow, and she was amused that they should be puzzled tonight.

She went back to her father, and the light of laughter had left her eyes. She asked: "What shall you do now?"

"What will he?"

"He will strive for peace. We may count surely on that."

"So he may. But it is plain that Cortéz is plotting war. That is why he killed those men here."

"Yes. I see that. I think Enrico does now. What I asked was, what shall you do?"

President Gómez answered only: "Yes. What?"

"You mean that you don't want me to know?"

"So I may. Or I may not be sure."

"Well, it is best that you should not say. I can't tell what I don't know. I must see what I can get Enrico to do."

CHAPTER THIRTY

AN INTERLUDE BETWEEN KISSES

"I HAVE been kissed enough," Juliana said. "Perhaps more. Suppose we talk sense for a change?"

"I have been talking the best sense in the world."

"Then I didn't hear. Do you know that the night is half gone, and we've talked of just nothing at all? What are you meaning to do?"

"This."

"You know I didn't mean that. I told you I'd been kissed enough. I want to know what you mean to do about the mess that we're in?"

"Clear out. I dislike the way they blow each other apart here. I prefer being alive with you."

"How do you mean to do that?"

"I don't mean to go back to San Cristóval. I don't like President Cortéz's ways, and I don't see why I should. We've too much to lose. We'll go by the *Billy Winch*."

Juliana frowned thoughtfully. It was a tempting idea. To get clear of all the mean murderous intrigue which is the rotten core of Central American politics. Why should Enrico risk his life in quarrels which were not his, and which were fought by rules that he did not know? As he had said, they had too much to lose.

"I thought," she temporised, "the *Billy Winch* was only a cargo-boat?"

"There are a few cabins for passengers. The captain would make you comfortable. And I might soon get you transferred to another ship."

"I shouldn't really mind about that. The question is whether we ought to go."

"What else can I do? We're not going to San Cristóval to help President Cortéz against Bioli and your father."

"You mean if he starts a war? No, we couldn't do that. But you could resign and stay here."

"Well, I'm willing to do that. I don't want to run away. But I don't think I should be much use. I don't understand their ways here, or I don't like them when I do."

"You might be more use for that."

"Perhaps you can say how?"

"Well, I did have an idea, but I don't say that it's any good; and it wasn't for if you stayed here. It was if I went with you to Baratá."

"You might say what it is."

So she did, at some length. It was an idea which Enrico admitted would never have entered his mind, which may have been another evidence of his failure to understand the political atmosphere to which he had come. But Juliana did not put it forward as more than a gambler's chance. Yet it was agreed at last, in the sanguine spirit of youth, that it was better than ignominious flight on the *Billy Winch*; it came to the time when they could put it in their minds as a settled thing.

"Don't you think," he asked, "that time for you to be kissed again?"

"Well," she said doubtfully, "if you could find any place where you haven' yet—"

Which was asking for what she got.

CHAPTER THIRTY-ONE

BIOLI WAITS FOR THE STORM

PRESIDENT GÓMEZ had the hard part of the man who waits. He had sent the body of Señor Philipo, and Señor Serati's more fragmentary remains, to San Cristóval, in coffins of the best quality. They were to have a state funeral there, and if President Cortéz should think fit to use the event for one of his patriotic orations, the hostilities which were already threatening might gain the fervour of a holy war.

He had held an enquiry into the circumstances of the tragedy, and had found out little that was not of a negative kind. Naturally, no one admitted placing a bomb. There had been an explosion at a time when the little party had been alone. The watchful military police had no doubt of that, though its inferences were not their business to say. They gave facts. It was a fact that there had been a bomb, for its fragments remained. These had some evidence of Bioli manufacture. There was no comfort in that.

Enrico and Juliana had left for San Cristóval. They had driven through crowded streets where many cheered and some scowled. The position was menacing and confused: no easier for those in the street than their rulers to read. Those who desired peace might cheer, seeing hope in the fact that their president's daughter went smiling to Baratá. It took some of the significance from the fact that the Legation of that country was vacant, and that its interests had been taken over by the Chilean envoy. Those who looked for war might see nothing better than that Juliana had married her country's foe, and left it in a black hour.

It was certain that Baratá, whether intending to attack Bioli, or give it nothing worse than a sharp fright, was acting in a most provocative manner.

Its frontier was closed. The usual twice-weekly mineral train had been turned back. The ferry across the estuary at San Cristóval had been stopped. Baratá's single destroyer, having loaded its torpedo-tubes with all possible publicity, had put out to sea. President Gómez was not greatly impressed by that. Indeed, it suggested to his mind that the whole affair was of the nature of a demonstration of force rather than preparation for actual war.

The *Esenda* would search long before it found any ship flying Bioli's ensign against which its torpedoes could be discharged, and the idea that it might molest the *Billy Winch* on the high seas was not seriously to be entertained. President Cortéz would not be crazy enough to interfere with a British ship. It would be too good to be true!

Meanwhile the *Billy Winch* had experienced an annoying delay. It had encountered a heavy gale, against which it had slowed down, and then, when it became worse, had lain-to, as the nature of its cargo, and its own venerable age, had required.

When the gale lessened, it would resume its course, and waddle sedately into San Luíz harbour. But that would be two days later than the hour when it had been expected to arrive. President Gómez, avoiding any overt preparation for war (as he had promised Enrico that he would do, so long as Bioli's frontiers were not violated, until at least twenty-four hours after his arrival at San Cristóval), thought that fate was unkind.

President Cortéz, giving orders for the reception of the returning envoy and his bride, looked at it in an opposite way. So the time passed until the presidential train, its brakes screeching noisily on its downhill course, bustled in to San Cristóval station, having made its journey in seventy-two minutes less than its previous record time, which had been considerably over thirty miles an hour; and Enrico and Juliana stepped out on to an empty platform, to see the shining bayonets of the soldiers who held its gates, and beyond them the countless heads of an excited, murmuring crowd.

CHAPTER THIRTY-TWO

PRESIDENT CORTÉZ AGREES TO HIS PRICE

PRESIDENT CORTÉZ had had a busy morning receiving the envoys of foreign powers who had called upon him on the instructions of their various governments, urging moderation and expressing their profound regret at a crime which had shocked the civilised world. They had all said the same things, and he had replied to them all in the same way. The offended dignity of Baratá must be vindicated, the requirements of international justice must be met. They would agree upon that. But so long as no further outrage should occur, so long as no provocative incident should render it impossible to restrain the natural indignation of a people whose generous emotions had been so deeply stirred, there would be no hasty action on his side. It was true that his envoy had been recalled. Could they blame him for that? Apart from other considerations, he wished to hear from his own lips his account of the tragedy in which he had been so nearly involved, and to have the benefit of his opinion concerning the intentions of the government of Bioli, whose good faith was so gravely suspected.

They received with approbation sentiments which they were bound to admire, and assurances which they were bound to accept. Knowing President Cortéz, they withdrew with dubious minds. But he would not have been troubled by that, even had their worst thoughts been an open page for him to read. It was sufficient that he played the game in a way they could not condemn.

It was true that he wished to reserve freedom of action until he had his envoy's report. Not that that would make any difference to him. If he were to hear anything he did not already know, it would be something which was not true, though it might be Dr. Dalston's honest belief. But he did wish to discover what that gentleman suspected or knew. He wished to handle the matter, if possible, so that he would secure his approval and co-operation in what he did.

By friendly means, if it could be done, but by any others which the occasion might require, he intended to secure the financial assistance to Baratá which Dr. Dalston was able, and had actually expressed, his intention to give. He had already thought of several ingenious paths (if the direct one should now be closed) to this desirable goal. He supposed that Dr. Dalston would value a bride so recently acquired. But could Baratá be expected to regard with equal complacency the presence of the daughter of President Gómez? Of a most obvious spy? There was for such a secure though unsavoury jail.

Enrico, who had planned to return to the hotel where he had spent so few hours before, found that matters were otherwise arranged. Not that there was any immediate threat of San Cristóval's jail either for Juliana or himself. They went from palace to palace. He was informed, as he stepped from the train, that President Cortéz would be honoured by the presence at his own Residency both of himself and his wife. But the intimation, however politely expressed, was conveyed as a settled thing, to which his consent was not required. If the soldiers who held back the crowds through which they drove were for their honour, it seemed excessive for an envoy returning under such circumstances; if for their security, their unpopularity must be judged to be very great. But it is evident that, if their orders be taken from others, those who guard may constrain. They felt as those whose freedom is pawned, for their own wits to redeem, if that be no more than they are able to do.

Arriving at their destination, they were shown to the suite which President Cortéz reserved for his most honoured guests. There was nothing ominous about that, nor in the excellent meal which was served to them there. After that, Enrico was informed that the President would receive him without further delay.

Juliana looked at him with eyes which tried to show more confidence than she was able to feel, now that the decisive moment had come.

"You'll do just as we agreed?" she asked, with the natural anxiety of one responsible for a plan which another must perform.

"Yes, you can count on that."

The idea had seemed fantastic when she had proposed it first, but her optimism had prevailed. It seemed more so now that the moment which would test its value had come.

He had told himself that she knew these people and their ways better than he, and that her judgment should be his guide. That had not ceased to be true, but he was about to play a card which would be fatal to them, if the suit were not the trumps which she had guessed it to be.

President Cortéz received his returned envoy with a gravity suitable to the occasion, and an affability suitable to the reception of a minister who had done well.

With more courtesy than he had considered appropriate for their first interview, he heaved his bulk out of the padded chair into which it had been sunk, and stepped forward to offer a fat but still muscular hand.

"I am glad," he said, "that you have come safely through a danger to which you should not have been exposed."

Enrico was tempted to reply that there had been little danger for him, but he remembered a resolution to let the President show his hand first, and he said only: "The wall protected Conradi and myself, so that we were in no danger at all."

"You might tell me just how it occurred."

Enrico did this in a colourless manner, endeavouring to give no indication of his own conclusions. He mentioned the fact that Conradi had gone first to the place where the explosion occurred, but without emphasising it. He did not advance it as a significant circumstance. He just mentioned facts.

He was prepared to be asked his opinion as to who was responsible for the crime, in which case his answer would have brought immediate crisis between himself and the man in whose power he was, but the question, when it came, after a pause of serious silence, as though the President were mentally weighing what he had heard, was framed in a different way: "What would you advise me to do?"

"So long as we have the assurance of President Gómez that he is exerting himself to the utmost to discover the criminal, and while he makes no move of any unfriendly nature, which I am sure he does not desire to do—"

"You are sure of that? You have married his daughter, as I must not forget."

"It was, in fact, as you may have heard, secretly done, without asking if he approved."

"Which he has since done?"

"Yes, but this unfortunate event made other questions seem less important than they might otherwise have been."

"Perhaps it did. But when you say he will do nothing of a provocative kind, do you forget that cargo of munitions that he has bought? For whom is it intended, if not for us? Is there no-provocation there?"

"That is more than I should care to deny. But he would say that it was bought before the present friendly negotiation began."

"So that he is now prepared for you to divert it to another port?"

"So he might be, if it were part of a bargain of settled peace."

"But you could do it, apart from that, which would be a service to Baratá?"

"I might have the power, but its importance, even if it should seem a right thing to do, might not be much, for I have his promise that he will not now be the one to commence a war."

President Cortéz became silent. He was quite shrewd enough to observe that there had been no real cordiality in Enrico's replies. He was unsure how much of the truth he might know or guess, or how far it might have biased his mind. He still hoped to see the fortune which was so temptingly in sight invested under his control. He did not wish to press this request of changing the destination of the *Billy Winch* to a point at which he would risk being faced by a blank refusal. Rather, he preferred to show that it was unimportant to him, he having another plan.

"It does not matter," he said, "I have dealt with that. Before it can arrive, we shall have landed a sufficient force in San Luíz to ensure that those munitions shall come into better hands than they were intended to reach."

"That would be to make war inevitable."

"Not at all. It will make it very foolish for them to fight. They are much fewer than we, and we shall have the modern arms on which they have depended for our defeat. We shall tell the world that we have taken that action explicitly to prevent a war. If our soldiers—I will tell you that they are embarking now, in every vessel we have been able to requisition—meet with no resistance, they will do violence to none, and they will evacuate San Luíz when the cargo has been secured."

"And after that you would give Bioli the benefit of the treaty I have negotiated with them?"

"After what has occurred? It would be effrontery to ask! If we allow things to go on as they were, with no more indemnity than Bioli will be able to pay, we shall have acted to an enemy in our power with a moderation the whole world must approve."

"I do not know that I should. I should ask first by whom, and by whose orders, the bomb was thrown."

President Cortéz stared. This was a straighter challenge than he had expected to meet, and he saw in his opponent's eyes that he realised all the implications of what he said. But he felt the game to be too entirely in his own hands to be much disturbed. If matters could not be smoothly arranged, there were other ways.

"And what," he asked, "should you say would be the answer to that?"

"I should say that Conradi could answer that better than I."

"And what would that answer be?"

"He would say that he is in the service of Baratá."

"Should you say the same?"

"I may still be in the service of Baratá. I should not serve you personally, if you mean that. I have a proposal to make."

President Cortéz heard this uncompromising reply with a grim mouth, but he controlled his anger to say: "You can propose what you will."

"I propose to give you a cheque for twenty thousand pounds which will be payable on your personal application at the counter of my London bank, on condition that you nominate me as your successor here."

The President heard this audacious offer with a countenance from which all expression had disappeared. It would have been evidence, to anyone who knew him, that he recognised that there might be a serious trial of strength where he had expected an easier victory. Behind that blank mask he considered the offer he had received with a favour which went far to justify Juliana's judgment. He had already amassed a considerable fortune, the bulk of which was invested safely in Europe and the United States. He had held his present office for a longer period than most American presidents find it healthy to do, and the time when he would take an eastern voyage from which he would not return could not, in prudence, be much longer delayed. An extra £20,000, however acquired, would round off those perilously accumulated gains in a most satisfactory manner, and make it foolish to continue to run the risks of the precarious eminence he now occupied. But so, also, would a larger sum.

"The offer," he said, "is most interesting, but you misapprehend the position in which you stand.

"I arrested you less than a fortnight ago on information laid by Señor Serati that you were a Bioli spy. I generously accepted your denial of that accusation, and I gave you an opportunity of proving your loyalty to this country which you had professed an intention to make your own.

"What is the result? Señor Serati is dead under circumstances which throw particular suspicion upon yourself, for you were one of the two who were close at hand when he was killed. Whether or not Conradi bad any part in those murders I cannot say. It may be known only to him and you. But that you have been serving Bioli, even while you have been our accredited representative there, is proved (if further proof were required) by the marriage which you have just made. We have prisons for spies. We have firing-squads for traitors, as you most certainly are. Your life, if you value it at so much, will cost you twenty thousand pounds. That of your wife, who has also come here as an evident spy, will cost you the same amount; or if you think her worth less, her father may be disposed to make up the amount. I shall jail you both, but on the payment of those sums you will be allowed to escape by a door which will not be properly locked, and from that day you will find that Baratá will be unhealthy for you.

"You can, of course, assault me if you will, as we are alone together, and for all I know you may be armed, but my foot is now on a bell which will summon the guards outside the door, by whom you would be bayoneted within less than the three minutes which I am giving you to decide what you will do."

"You mean that I shall be arrested as a spy unless I agree to give you twenty thousand pounds, and my wife's liberty will cost me the same amount?"

"The question is not of liberty, but of life, and the three minutes is starting now." As he said this President Cortéz pulled out his watch.

"You can put that back, for I can answer you in a shorter time. My offer may change, but it certainly will not increase. I will tell you this. Before leaving San Sebastián I made a sworn declaration before the British Consul there of my experiences since I landed on this continent, and of the circumstances under which my two colleagues died. I added that I appreciated the risk I took in returning here, and gave instructions for the document to be published throughout the world, if any harm should happen to me. It is on the way by airmail to London now."

"You think it will be a tale which would be believed?"

"Yes, for my reputation is known, and I should have no motive to lie. Besides that, I was handed Señor Philipo's pocket-book when he died, and some of its contents have gone by the same route."

The last statement was literally true, but was not free from an element of bluff, for Señor Philipo had been a most cautious man. The contents of his wallet had been curious enough, but, apart from one document of doubtful interpretation, had included no reference whatever to the occurrences with which Dr. Dalston had been concerned. But how was President Cortéz to know that?

After a mere second of hesitation he asked: "If I accept your offer, what will become of those documents?"

"I shall cable, immediately that you have left this country, for the envelope which contains them to be destroyed with its seals unbroken."

"If you will make it twenty-five thousand, I will agree."

"My offer was twenty thousand. It is in grave danger of being reduced to eighteen."

"Well, I agree. But you will find Conradi a useful man."

"He will be useful to hang, as an example for other rogues. But when he learns I am in control, I suppose he will not stay to find out what I shall be likely to do."

"I suppose not. Your wife and you will do me the honour of dining with me tonight?"

"Yes, I am sure she will be pleased."

"I should say that you owe much to her."

"I owe more than you can suppose."

"Well, we will say no more upon business which is done. You will like me to recall the troops which are embarking now?"

"It will save useless expense. I am content that we say no more, except upon details which must be arranged tomorrow. But I will tell you this. I have been your friend. For I have given you a longer life than you would have had here."

"I have kept it till now. I have no reason to think I might not have done so a longer time."

"I was not thinking of that. Your blood pressure is far too high."

President Cortéz said nothing to this. It was a free medical opinion which coincided with others he had obtained at a higher price.

CHAPTER THIRTY-THREE

A PALACE IS BOUGHT AND SOLD

IT is a common experience that those of us who can face adversity with unflinching eyes will become frightened when all goes well, or when a great joy is very nearly within our grasp, lest we should become the sport of the mocking fates, and find that we have been shown that which we shall never hold in our living hands; and it was so that Juliana's confidence faltered as the day closed that had seen the success of the audacious plan which she had proposed, and on which they had risked so much.

The dinner, at which she and Enrico had been the President's only guests, had been a very pleasant successful meal.

With an aspect of good spirits, which may have been genuine enough, their host had entertained them with a stream of complimentary and anecdotal conversation, which included many items of incidental information such as might be useful to the man whom he had undertaken, by whatever political devices, to introduce to his own position, while avoiding any direct reference to the business deal which had been verbally agreed less than an hour before.

It was only as they were about to rise that he had said, in a casual tone: "By the way, you will need this Residency for your own use. I can rely that you will purchase it at a fair price?"

It was a question which Enrico had not considered. He had not known—actually did not know now—whether it were the property of President Cortéz, or of the State, the latter ownership being the more probable, though the distinction—in Baratá—might not be easy to make.

He had vaguely supposed that the £20,000 he was to pay for the goodwill of the presidential office was an inclusive and final figure, as he had meant it to be. If he were wrong, he would be prepared, within reason, to amend his price, but he had no intention of being fleeced.

"I will do what is fair," he said. "But palaces must be rather difficult to sell at anything better than bargain rates. There is, I suppose, no more than a limited demand for them in Baratá. I will get an estate agent to value it, after you have left, and I will pay whatever he may declare to be due to you."

President Cortéz said, with no sign of dissatisfaction at a decision which put forward the valuation to a date on which the agent might be more concerned to please the new president than the old, and which reserved the question of ownership in so clear and yet unexceptionable a phrase: "That is all I ask, for I know you will do what is fair, in your English way."

"So," Enrico replied, "you may be sure that I shall."

"But," he remarked to Juliana, when they had reached the secure solitude of the sumptuous bed-chamber which President Cortéz reserved for his most favoured guests, "I should say that it has cost a small fortune to fit this place up in the way he has, and I wish he had not tied me down by making it a point of honour to pay. I should call him the cleverest rascal I have ever met."

"Yes, I can see how you felt. But all the same, I was rather glad."

"I don't see why you—"

"Well, I was. It made it seem more real somehow. If he hadn't honestly meant to leave you here in his place, he wouldn't have troubled to drive that bargain... The fact is, however silly it sounds, that it's been so easy that I've been afraid."

"Afraid of what?"

"Afraid, even now, that he may find some way to plot your death and his own return."

"Do you think he'll like to do that? I don't know. I gave him a hint about his blood-pressure that might turn his mind another way.

"But there's another hint I might give him. English banks won't pay cheques after the death of the man who draws them. That ought to secure me a position of particular safety for a few weeks, so far as his influence goes, and after that— Is it not possible that Baratá may prefer a president who spends, and who at least tries to give them a fair deal, to one who takes, and only looks after himself and his own gang?"

It was a question to be answered only in the years to come, being a tale that is not yet told.

But the moment, at least, was theirs.

ABOUT THE AUTHOR

SYDNEY FOWLER WRIGHT (1874-1965) penned over seventy volumes of science fiction, fantasy, classic mysteries, historical novels, poetry, and non-fiction, many of them being published by the Borgo Press Imprint of Wildside Press.

www.ingramcontent.com/pod-product-compliance
Lightning Source LLC
Chambersburg PA
CBHW020445270626
47155CB00022B/1679